THE ADVENTURES OF A
AND OTHI

To Christine

With my love and best wishes

Nigel

In memory of my dear Lorna, my wife of nearly fifty-nine years, who passed away while this book was in publication.

THE ADVENTURES OF AN ELDERLY GENTLEMAN AND OTHER STORIES

Nigel Power

ARTHUR H. STOCKWELL LTD
Torrs Park, Ilfracombe, Devon, EX34 8BA
Established 1898
www.ahstockwell.co.uk

British Library Cataloguing-in-Publication Data.
A catalogue record for this book is available
from the British Library.

ISBN 978-0-7223-5151-2
Printed in Great Britain by
Arthur H. Stockwell Ltd
Torrs Park   Ilfracombe
Devon EX34 8BA

CONTENTS

PARTLY OLD

He assumed he must be old. His family and friends seemed to think so, but they hadn't got as far as using adjectives such as 'ancient' or 'vintage'. He didn't feel old. True, he had passed his eighty-fifth birthday, but he had decided to live until he was at least 100. Admittedly, his hearing was not as good as it had been when he was younger, and he often couldn't hear what his granddaughters said to him. His eyesight, however, since he had had his cataracts done, was better than it had been for many years. He didn't need any support when he went for a walk and his teeth were all his own. Although there was a lift between his floor and ground level he made a point of using the stairs at least once a day, when he went down to collect his paper. Perhaps he was just 'partly old'. Yes, he'd accept that.

He hadn't liked the idea of moving out of his house, but the flat – no! he mustn't call it that – the apartment his children had found for him had much to commend it. It had four rooms – living room, bedroom, kitchen and bathroom – with a small south-facing balcony off the living room. The views across the valley were splendid, and from his position high up on a south-facing hillside he could see for miles. On a clear day, with the binoculars (or should he call them field glasses?) given him by two of his grandchildren, he could see for several miles, east, south and west. He had bought an Ordnance Survey map and spent many a pleasant hour identifying farms and landmarks as well as three villages that he could see from his window. In each of the three villages he could see their churches in prominent positions, two with spires and one with a tower. He could watch traffic on a dual carriageway making its way towards a town on the south coast; and away to his right, the west, he could see trains on the hourly cross-country service. He knew the media delighted in quoting comments of members of the public about poor timekeeping on the rail network, but his little trains, as he liked to call them, always seem to be spot on time.

The patchwork of fields interested him. The farms he could see seemed to operate a mixed economy with both arable and pasture farming. The fields of oilseed rape had almost lost their golden sheen and those grown with grass were being harvested, with tractors and trailers busy removing the cuttings from early morning till after dusk. In the fields with livestock he could see horses, cattle and sheep; in a field to the west he could see deer – he assumed that they must be at Bucklands Farm, if he had matched the fields to his map correctly.

With his field glasses he delighted in looking at the wildlife, particularly the birds. The summer visitors had now arrived and the house martins put on some spectacular aerial displays. He was sure that there was a nest above one of his windows which was visited regularly – not just by two birds, but by several, one after another. Earlier, in spring, he had watched blackbirds, robins and a thrush collecting nesting materials, while further away he had seen rooks and jackdaws flying by with twigs in their beaks as they built high in the trees in a copse in the valley to his left. Also in the copse he had noticed woodpeckers, both green and spotted, hammering at the trunks of trees and, even with his poor hearing, he had been able to detect the rhythmic beat as they worked rapidly. Why it didn't give them headaches he couldn't imagine. Now it was feeding time and he could detect many small birds diving into the hedges with offerings for the young that hadn't yet fledged. Various titmice, including gatherings of long-tailed tits, were especially busy. Sparrows, dunnocks, chaffinches, the pretty goldfinches and others he couldn't identify but which he classified as LBJs (little brown jobbies) were all intent on the same mission of filling empty stomachs. He had no difficulty seeing his friendly blackbird, who came regularly for the raisins he put on the balcony, before flying on to his singing perch on the tree just below his window. Recently, a robin had started coming for the mealworms he put out.

On this beautiful morning, a Thursday, there would be a few farmers' stalls in the village. It was no more than a ten-minute walk away, even at his deliberate pace, and he might be able to buy a trout fillet for his lunch. He would like to make some parsley sauce to go with the trout, but now that he no longer had a garden he did not have access to fresh parsley, unless there was a vegetable stall with herbs for sale. He spent a few minutes wondering if there was anything else he needed to get while he was out. Then, taking a shopping bag and remembering to put on his shoes – more than once he had gone out in his slippers – he locked his door, and set off down the stairs and out of the main entrance.

It really was a lovely day, warm with just a gentle breeze. Even though it was still quite early, there were several people about, some of whom he recognised. Most of them greeted him with comments about the loveliness of the day. There were five stalls and he was able to buy fish and a bunch of fresh parsley. He also bought two pieces of local cheese and treated himself to a small box of chocolates made by the chocolatier in the neighbouring town.

On his way back he made a diversion into the local park and walked round the small lake where the ducks were standing on their heads, pecking at the weed under the water. He was then delighted to spot a pair of grebes that he hadn't seen there before. As he walked on he just had to stop and admire the roses. The warm sun inspired them to give off their perfume, which brought back memories of the roses he had grown.

Coming out of the park he decided to sit on a bench which afforded a view of the rising ground to the north of the village. There was little traffic on this minor road, which eventually wound its way through the valley he could see from his windows. He saw one very brightly polished car go past and noted that the three letters on its number plate were DOG. When, half a minute later, a car with the letters FOX passed by he wondered what might be next – would there be a CAT or a HOG? No, the next one was JXX, but the one behind it had EAD on its number plate. Now, he thought, you could make a word with those letters by adding another. So he began exploring the possibilities. Head, dead, mead. The first two rhymed, but not with the third. But what about lead and read. They would rhyme with all of them, as you could say them both ways. When you read a book, rhyming with reed, and get to the end you will have read it, rhyming with red.

He was thinking about leading an animal or swinging the lead when he was interrupted by someone shouting. A tatty van had pulled up and the passenger was trying to attract his attention.

'Hey, mate,' the man called, 'is this the way to Coltsford?'

He got up and went over to the van.

'Yes, this road will take you to Coltsford, but if you are not familiar with the road, be careful: there are one or two sharp bends, especially by the deer farm.'

'Did you say deer farm? Thanks, old man – we'll look out for it.'

Old man! He didn't think much of that.

Turning to the driver, the man in the van said, with a note of excitement in his voice, 'Did ye hear that, Al? A deer . . .'

The rest was lost in an explosion of noise from the engine and a belch of smoke from the exhaust as with creaks, groans and rattles the van went on its way. The vehicle had clearly had previous owners as part of its original light-blue paint had been overpainted with dark blue, presumably covering up some original lettering. He looked after it and could just distinguish PYO on the number plate.

'Hmm!' he thought. 'What could you do with PYO?'

The first thing that came into his head was 'Pick Your Own'. That reminded him of strawberries in the fields. Maybe they were farmers, but he thought that unlikely. Now, what else could you do with these letters? 'Spyhole' would work, but P followed by Y needed an H in between – then 'physiotherapy' or 'physiognomy'. Was there a word 'physiology'? If you didn't start with P, what other possibilities were there? 'Eponymous' – yes that worked. Now, what did it mean?

'Deep in thought, Jim?' said a voice.

Looking up, he saw his friend Ben standing beside him.

'Good morning, Ben. What a lovely day! I've been up to the village and I thought I'd sit here and look at the scenery and watch the traffic.'

'Still looking at car numbers and making words out of them?'

'Yes! Today I saw a DOG followed by a FOX.'

'That can't be right,' smiled Ben. 'The dog usually chases the fox in hunting, not the other way around.'

'Hey, that's good. I hadn't thought of that. But we had a decrepit old van pull up a few minutes back. Did you see it – light blue with a great daub of dark-blue paint on its side?'

'I did see it, just disappearing in a cloud of smoke. Where was it going?'

'They asked the way to Coltsford. I don't know if it was a farm vehicle, or perhaps they were scrap-metal merchants.'

'What, driving some of the scrap they had collected!' laughed Ben. 'Any road up, I'm glad I've met you. My two grandsons are playing cricket for the village on Saturday over at Marchington and my son is going to take me to watch them. Do you feel like joining us?'

'This Saturday – yes, that would be grand as both my families will be away, one on holiday and the others have been invited to a wedding. If this weather holds it will be a very pleasant way to spend the afternoon. What time and where?'

'We'll pick you up outside your apartment around one thirty. Can you manage that?'

'No problem. Thanks for inviting me. But I'd better be going now – I've sat here long enough and I've some fish to cook.'

So saying, he made his way home, but before putting his purchases away and starting his cooking he went out on to his balcony. The countryside was basking in the sunshine, but there was plenty of activity. Vehicles on the dual carriageway were reflecting the sun as they sped on their way to he knew not where. He knew where the little birds were going though as they flew directly into gaps in the hedges. Looking to the west, with his field glasses, he was surprised to see the tatty old van parked in a gateway just round the corner from the deer farm. Perhaps it had broken down. He felt a little uneasy about seeing the van there, although he couldn't think why.

After lunch, he sat in his chair facing his view and picked up his daily national newspaper, but before long the paper fell on to the floor as he drifted off into his afternoon nap. He hadn't even turned to the puzzle page or the letters, which were often more interesting than the news items, which were nearly all opinion or speculation. Nearly an hour later he was startled awake by the phone ringing. Fortunately, it was within reach. On answering it he discovered it was a grandson checking that he was all right and inviting him to Sunday lunch, when they would tell him all about the wedding. He was given instructions about the time he was to be ready to be picked up.

Now that he was awake, he made himself a cup of tea and then decided to look at the local paper he had bought in the morning. He didn't have a newspaper every day, but he felt he ought to try to keep up to date by buying a copy occasionally. There were articles in which local councillors were pontificating on plans for development of the area and the need for more houses to be built on the edges of villages, summaries of national news and accounts of road accidents, village fairs and garden parties. As he turned the pages his attention was caught by an account of sheep being stolen from a couple of farms. Police were appealing for witnesses or information about the rustlers. He wondered if any of the farms he could see from his windows had been affected.

In the evening there was nothing to interest him on television after he had listened to the news, so he sat and listened to the birds outside his window. He wished he was able to identify all the different songs they sang, but there were so many it really was a chorus with a blackbird taking the role of lead soloist. Although he began to feel drowsy, his mind was still active as he thought about the sheep rustling that had also been featured on the regional television news.

It was still light, being so close to the longest day, when he went to bed, but it wasn't long before he was asleep. It seemed only a few minutes before he woke again, although it was beginning to get light. He looked at his clock, which showed ten to five. He felt something must have woken him, so he lay in bed not moving and listening attentively. Then he heard a scratching that seemed to be coming from the living room. He got out of bed and went to look for the cause of the noise and discovered that he hadn't shut the window next to the door on to the balcony, and there was the blackbird on the balcony tapping his beak on the window sill and waiting for his raisins.

He could not deny such a friendly cheeky companion, so he fetched the raisin jar and went out on to the balcony. It was quite warm, even though it was not yet fully light. He put some raisins on the balustrade and he thought he would just have a look at the countryside before going back to bed. There was a steady stream of traffic on the main road, including a couple of cars towing caravans towards the coast – early arrivals on a Friday before the weekend rush. Everywhere else everything seemed quiet. He couldn't see any activity in the villages, but some of the grazing animals were having an early breakfast. As he turned from looking east and south to view how far the sun had reached in the west he saw there was movement in a distant field.

His interest aroused, he retrieved his binoculars from their shelf in the living room. Yes, it looked like that old light-blue van in the drive to Bucklands Farm and men and dogs chasing the deer. Two men were with the dogs and one man was by the doors of the van. And now the man opened the doors as the other men cornered a deer and pushed it into the van. As he watched, the procedure was repeated. Were these people the rustlers the police were after? Hastily he went back inside, and found his phone and the local paper: he was sure there was a number for the police at the end of the article about sheep stealing. Yes, there it was. He went back on to the balcony while he phoned the number. There was a reply immediately.

'Sergeant Cartwright, Moleshire Police – how can I help you?'

'I think I might be able to help you. I think there might be some deer rustling going on at the moment. I can see it from my window.'

'Please can you give me some details? Where do you think this is happening?'

'Bucklands Farm, near Coltsford.'

'Can you give me your name and where you are?'

'I am James Willoughby and I live at Cloverhill Court at—'

The Sergeant interrupted: 'I know – my aunt lived in one of the apartments until about six months ago.'

'I wouldn't have met her – I've only been here about four months.'

'Then you may have moved into her apartment. It has a magnificent panoramic view of the valley'.

'That's right – Number 4. It is a wonderful view. I don't normally look out at this time of the morning, only the blackbird woke me up looking for raisins.'

'Oh, he's still at it, is he? Auntie will be so pleased he has found a new friend. Mr Willoughby, I've sent an alert out to a couple of patrols, and they are making their way to the area. Can you give me any more information?'

'Yes, it's an old light-blue long transit-type vehicle with large splodges of dark-blue paint on the sides where the previous owner's name must have been. Perhaps 'clapped-out' is a good description of its condition. I saw it yesterday when I was asked if they were on the right road for Coltsford. I told them to be careful on the road as there are some nasty bends, especially near the deer farm. I wasn't sure they would be able to negotiate the bends in that van, but they seemed to get excited when I mentioned the deer farm. I saw them later from my window stopped in a gateway near the farm.'

'Thank you. Can you tell us anything else about the van?'

'Oh, I nearly forgot: the reg number contains the letters PYO – I thought, at the time, of "Pick Your Own" and wondered if it was a farm vehicle.'

'That's very helpful. Full marks for observation. Can you still see them, Mr Willoughby? Are they still there?'

'Yes, they are. Wait a moment – they have shut the doors. It looks as though they are calling the dogs and they have jumped into the front of the van. I think they are about to go. Yes, they must have started the engine – there is a great cloud of dirty black smoke – surely, that must be illegal – and they're moving.'

'Can you see which way they are going?'

'I'm watching to see which way. . . . Ah! They have turned towards Coltsford and I shall lose sight of them soon, but if they stay on the same road I should see them go over the railway bridge, although only briefly as there are some big trees on that road. Oh, I can see a police car just down below me on the Coltsford road. The van is now out of my view.'

'There should soon be another patrol approaching from Coltsford. We need to know if the van keeps on the same road.'

'This is like being the "eye in the sky". Yes! There it is, approaching the railway bridge now. More black smoke as it climbs the hill to the bridge.'

'Thank you, Mr Willoughby. The chase is on now, and hopefully we shall catch them. I will let you know how it goes. You can go back to bed now. Sleep well.'

He switched off the phone and went back to bed. He didn't know if he would be able to sleep after all that excitement. However, the next thing he knew there was a bright light in his room as the rays of the sun pierced through a gap in the curtains. Time to get up.

The morning was much as usual – he made his breakfast of scrambled egg on toast, went downstairs, collected his paper and fed the birds. He chose a ready meal from his freezer for his dinner, and put it in the oven. When it was cooked, he put the television on for the news and sat down to his meal. The very first item on the regional news was that suspects had been detained early in the morning on suspicion of stealing sheep and other animals. The police had acted on observations supplied by an elderly resident who was alerted by some strange behaviour at dawn. 'Elderly' was the adjective used – much better than 'old'.

He heard the rest of the news and then switched the box off and went though to the kitchen to wash up. The buzzer sounded, suggesting that he had a visitor.

He picked up the intercom to ask who was there, and a voice answered 'It's Sergeant Cartwright – we spoke early this morning. Can I come up?'

'Wait a moment and I'll let you in.'

When Sergeant Cartwright had been let in, she said, 'Its lovely to meet you, Mr Willoughby. I wanted to call and thank you for your help this morning. It was a very successful operation. You were right about the van being clapped out: it broke down shortly after it passed over the railway bridge. Our patrols arrived at the same time from opposite directions and we were able to arrest all three miscreants. They couldn't do otherwise than admit that they had taken the deer without permission, although they were prepared to deny all knowledge of sheep theft until one of them said he wasn't with them when they stole the sheep. They aren't a very bright bunch. We phoned the farmer: he hadn't heard anything, but he came with a tractor and trailer and was able to rescue all the deer. A few had superficial wounds and dog bites, but all will survive. He was most grateful and asked me to pass on his thanks to you. He said he would like to phone and thank you himself – do you mind if I give him your number? Now, I have an ulterior motive for visiting rather than just phoning: I'd like to feast my eyes on your lovely view for a moment.'

'Many thanks for coming and giving me that information. I am so pleased the deer are safe. Now, if you have time for a cup of tea, I'll put the kettle on and you can sit on the balcony and look at the countryside. The blackbird might even come to see you – he often calls after lunch.'

When the tea was served, Sergeant Cartwright said, 'James, you must have very good eyesight. I can hardly see Bucklands Farm from here.'

'Ah, but the sun has moved round and it is not highlighting the west as it was early this morning. Try these.' And he passed her the field glasses.

'That's much better. I can see the railway bridge and – my lucky day – there's a train just coming through. I had better go and find my bed. I'm on duty again at 11 p.m. tonight. There may be more news when I get back to the station. The thieves will get their day in court, but I think they will plead guilty, so we won't need you as a witness. They'll be charged with animal theft and a string of motoring offences. The van isn't taxed or insured, the driver hasn't a licence and the vehicle isn't roadworthy. We think they were taking the animals to a slaughterhouse near Birmingham. Our West Midlands colleagues have been concerned about that place for some time. So goodbye, and many thanks again. It has been a privilege to meet you. You're a valuable member of society.'

After the police officer had departed, he felt it was time he had a nap. Such excitement was enough to last him a month, and he wanted to be able to keep awake the following afternoon at the cricket.

He woke to the phone ringing.

'Mr Willoughby?' said a strange voice. 'Sam Small from Bucklands Farm here. I just had to ring and thank you for your great detective work. I never heard a sound during the night, and had you not seen what was happening to my herd I would have lost twenty-five of them. I count myself very fortunate. I have spoken to some of my colleague farmers and they are delighted that that gang has been caught. We reckon you deserve a medal or an award or something.'

'That's very kind of you, Mr Small. I am glad you didn't lose any of your animals and I hope none was badly injured. Have they all recovered from their ordeal?'

'Well, they all seem to be eating well, although a couple have injuries I need to keep an eye on. Do you eat venison, Mr Willoughby?'

'I do, Mr Small. I live alone, but often have meals with my son or daughter and their families.'

'Splendid. I'll send some prime cuts that you can share with your families. Perhaps they'll cook them for you. Let me have your address and I'll see to it.'

'That is most kind. A much better outcome for us than for those crooks!'

He had hardly put the phone down when it rang again. This time it was his friend Ben, checking he was still up for going to cricket the following day.

Then Ben said, 'Did you hear that the sheep stealers have been caught near Coltsford? Do you think that old van we saw yesterday was involved? Did you see it again?'

He told Ben he had seen it in a gateway near the farm later that morning, then assured him he would be ready on the following day.

17

He thought he might make himself a sandwich before the early evening news came on, but he was only halfway through that task when the phone rang again. He couldn't remember when last he had so many calls in one day.

As soon as he picked it up and said 'Hello' a voice replied, 'Hello, Grandad. It's Phil. We're at the airport waiting for our flight to be called, and Dad and Holly have gone to look for something to read on the plane. Are you all right?'

Before he could say more than 'Yes', his grandson went on: 'I've just seen on my phone that the police have caught those sheep stealers. Apparently, they were spotted by some old geezer who couldn't sleep. Got to go – the others have just come back. I'll take some pictures of Malta to show you. Over and out. Bye.'

He sat still for a few minutes thinking he might be old, or partly old, but he could still be useful. The Sergeant said he was a valuable member of society. It gave him a warm glow. But OLD GEEZER indeed!

AN ARRESTING SUMMER'S OUTING

James Willoughby woke to hear rain drumming on his bedroom window. He looked at his bedroom clock and was relieved to discover that it was not yet four o'clock; so he had time to go back to sleep in the hope that the rain would stop by the time he had to get up. When he woke again three hours later the sun was shining through a gap in his curtains. When he checked his clock he realised that it was a Saturday and the 4th of July. Why did that date sound special? Of course – American Independence Day. Oh well – it wasn't special as far as he was concerned, but he was pleased that it was Saturday, the sun was shining and there would be plenty of daylight.

'Well, James,' he said to himself 'we had better get up and enjoy this July day. At your age of eighty-five you had better make the best of such days left to you.'

So saying, he got out of bed, put on his slippers and went through to the bathroom to have a shave and a shower. Then, just in dressing gown and slippers, he went through to the kitchen to make his next decision – what to have for breakfast. The decision after breakfast would be what to wear. He would make himself scrambled egg on toast and, he decided after an argument with himself, a grilled rasher of bacon.

Having had breakfast and washed up, he went through to his living room on the way back to his bedroom, but stopped to open the curtains and go out on to his small balcony. Still wearing just his dressing gown, he could look out over the valley below him to east, south and west without being overlooked himself. This was the great advantage of living in an apartment on the second floor of the block located on a south-facing hillside. He liked to watch the birds that had been busy for several hours already and check that all the farm animals were grazing peacefully. The road to the coast, twenty miles away, was already busy (probably had been since before dawn) with holiday traffic. He left a few raisins for his friendly blackbird neighbour and some mealworms for the robin, then continued to his bedroom.

He had remembered to check his calendar for appointments before deciding what to wear. Today, his friend Ben and Ben's son Mark would call for him immediately after lunch to take him to the cricket match fifteen miles away, in which Ben's grandsons Josh and Dave would be playing. When he had dressed he left his flat and went down the stairs, avoiding the lift (worth a pat on the back), to fetch his newspaper from the entrance hall. After a few words of greeting with one of the other residents, he retraced his steps, again avoiding the lift (worth another pat on the back), and spent the next half an hour reading the paper. The main headline reported a massive drugs capture by a Border Force patrol boat two miles from a port in the next county. The drugs had a street value of several million pounds. They may not have seized the complete haul – there was a suspicion that some had been transferred to another vessel while still at sea and before the arrest had been effected.

There was also a report of new cases of coronavirus in two African countries. As he put the paper down he wondered how he would fare being locked down in the apartment that had been his home for less than a year. On the plus side, he had his wonderful panoramic view with continuous action to watch, but on the debit side he now had no garden of his own to work or laze in.

He spent the rest of the morning on a few minor tasks and then prepared a light lunch of soup and cake. The soup was watercress, and it had been made by one of the lovely ladies who regularly checked on his health and well-being. He was very lucky, and most appreciative of the kindness of his four 'girlfriends', who ensured that he never felt lonely or forgotten, especially if they knew his family were unable to visit. He made sure that if he baked some bread rolls he made sufficient to share with one or two of the 'girls'. He thought of them as girls even though a couple were older than he.

He was ready when Ben and Mark called for him. They explained that today's match was a friendly with no league points at stake; so while it would still be very competitive, it should also be good-humoured. The fixture between the teams went back many years, and honours were about even. As the weather was fine after the overnight showers, they anticipated that there would be a good crowd from both villages. Also, as the ground was adjacent to a busy road, but set well back from the road with plenty of car-parking space, they expected that some passing motorists would stop for a while and watch the match from their cars.

When they arrived at the ground and parked behind the pavilion, Ben was quick to spot three seats in a good viewing position.

He called, 'Come on, Jim – we are in luck. There are three good seats just over there. We'll keep one for Mark. I expect he will want to see if his boys have arrived safely. One or possibly both are bringing their girlfriends with them.'

The match was due to start in ten minutes, so while they waited James had a good look around, noting the positions of the stumps (already pitched but bail-less), the outfield and boundaries and the cars parked along the opposite side of the ground with some spectators sitting in them. The pitch itself and the square looked as though it had recently been mown, but the grass of the outfield looked green and lush, having benefitted from the overnight rain.

There was a ripple of applause as the umpires and captains emerged from the pavilion to walk on to the pitch, where a coin was tossed to decide who would bat first. It appeared that the hosts were going to have the first innings.

As the visitors took to the field followed by the home team's opening batsmen, James, Ben and Mark settled down to watch. James had already noted the trees beyond the road in full leaf stirred just a little by a slight breeze, which tempered the heat of the sun and, to his mind, contributed to a quintessentially typical English country scene.

The batting side made steady progress, but James thought that the scoring rate was quite slow.

He remarked to Ben, 'Have you noticed how few balls are getting to the boundary? Shots that should have been worth four are being chased and caught by the fielders and restricted to two runs. Too much grass has been left on the outfield, and it is slowing the ball.'

Ben replied, 'Yes, there have been some good strokes played that didn't get the reward they should have. This is likely to be a low-scoring match, I think. What do you think of the player facing the bowling now?'

'He has a good technique, a good upright stance, and has played some good shots. He is better playing off the back foot, but sometimes doesn't use his feet sufficiently when the ball is pitched up and so doesn't quite get to the pitch of it, with the result that he is inclined to 'spoon' it up. Watch him this over. He has played back to three balls with good shots but all to fielders. Now, there you are – caught in the covers. He started to go back, then came forward, didn't get to the pitch of the ball and scooped it up to be caught. Let's see how many he made.'

'I see what you mean. Ah, the score's up now! He scored 29 and the total is now 52 for three. Honours about even at this point, I think,' said Ben.

A few more runs had been scored and the total had reached 69 for three when Mark and Ben exclaimed, 'Josh is going to bowl! We must watch this.'

James leaned forward and turned to Mark: 'His mother's not here to watch him?'

'No, she's on duty nursing at the hospital today. A pity – she likes to watch the boys play.'

They watched Josh's first over. The first ball was a long hop, hit to the boundary; the next four brought no runs; and the last was hit for two. In his second over, three singles were scored.

Ben turned to James: 'Well, Jim, any comments?'

'Quite a nice action. Occasionally he drops his leading shoulder in his delivery stride and concedes runs, but when he stands a little taller the batsmen have to be careful.'

The score had reached 83 for three when Josh bowled a ball that took the outside edge of the bat and was caught by the keeper. The score became 83 for four.

'Exactly the delivery he has been trying to bowl,' commented James. 'Shoulder up, ball left his hand a little higher and more attention given to accuracy and less to speed.'

In the next over Josh took another wicket. This was well caught at slip by his brother: 89 for five.

Enthusiastic applause, particularly by the boys' father and grandfather.

Ben chortled, 'That will look good in the score book – "caught D. Foster; bowled J. Foster". We could do with a few more like that.'

When the score had reached 123 for six, another bowling change was made.

Mark leaned across and said, 'Mr Willoughby, the new bowler is playing his first match with us. He is reputed to be a useful spin bowler. See what you think of him.'

James watched the new man bowl two overs and then said, 'From here I can't tell how accurate his direction is, but the length he bowls seems just about right and consistent. He is a bit square on when he delivers the ball. I wonder if he would be more sideways on if he bowled round the wicket. Oh, he is just going to do that.' The next ball clean-bowled the batsman and James commented, 'Spot on! Much better round the wicket. He will be pleased with that.'

The score was then 132 for seven.

Five runs later James exclaimed, 'Oh no. I don't think the umpire saw it.'

'What didn't he see?' asked Ben.

'There was a short run. In their eagerness to take two the non-striker didn't touch his bat down before going back for the second. The score should only have been credited one. I didn't see the umpire give any signal.'

'Is there a signal for a short run?' asked both Ben and Mark.

'Oh yes,' said James, and demonstrated by raising his right arm to the side and bringing his thumb up to his shoulder.

Another wicket fell. The score reached 148 and then an accident occurred. The ball was driven hard back, hit the bat of the non-striker before he could avoid it and ricocheted on to the head of the umpire, who staggered and collapsed. Mark, a paramedic, was out of his seat immediately and running on to the pitch to give assistance. After a few minutes the umpire was helped to his feet and professed that he felt all right to continue.

The end of the innings came fairly soon after the incident, when the hosts were all out for 156. The tea interval was signalled. Mark spent more time assessing the umpire while James and Ben enjoyed some refreshment and a chat with Josh and Dave and their girlfriends, Poppy and Lizzie. James took the opportunity to visit the toilet. When he got back there was news and a suggestion.

Mark had returned and had the two captains with him. Mark had advised that the injured umpire should not continue to officiate and the club secretary had taken him to A & E for a concussion check. This meant they were an umpire short. Would Mr Willoughby be willing to take his place?

James was somewhat stunned by the request, and he needed a moment or two to think before he responded.

'Oh dear!' said James. 'It's a long time since I last umpired and I don't have a licence. My eyesight's fine, but my hearing is a little weak. I suppose I am fairly neutral; although I came with the visitors, I don't have any real association with the club. Surely there is someone else.'

'As this is a friendly, you don't have to hold a licence,' said Mark. 'And you also know cricket and the rules, including the signal for a short run,' he added with a grin.

James looked at the two captains. 'Are you happy that I should substitute?'

Both looked at him and said, 'We should be delighted if you would stand.'

'OK,' said James, 'but you must just give me a revision course on the way batsmen ask for their guard when they come in to bat. Things may have changed since I last umpired.'

For the first over of the visitors' reply, James stood at square leg with his back to the pavilion, facing the cars parked along the opposite side of the ground. The first wicket fell with the score on 22, which brought Ben's grandson Dave in to bat. The score rose steadily until it reached 62 for two, which was when James was called on to make a judgement. Dave played a good on drive and set off for a run. He turned to come back for a second, but was well short of the crease when the keeper removed the bails. It was a very easy decision for James to make to give him run out, but he could not understand why Dave had chosen to go for such a risky run.

James looked around the ground in the direction in which the ball was played and then realised what must have happened. There was a small boy playing inside the boundary with a red ball. The match ball must have been held up by the lengthy grass in the outfield and Dave, when he looked to where he expected the ball to be, must have seen the little boy's red ball. While the new batsman was making his way to the crease James caught the eye of the other umpire, so that he didn't allow the game to continue. He walked over to where the small boy was playing and found the boy's mother. He advised her that playing inside the boundary was dangerous, and he said that with one accident already during the afternoon he didn't want to see her child hurt. Thereafter she kept her son and his ball well outside the boundary.

From 63 for three, when Dave was out, the score climbed to 129 for five. Then James had to make his next judgement and deal with a controversial situation. He was the umpire at the bowler's end when the batsman played the ball to a fielder, who threw it back to the keeper. The keeper failed to catch it, and the ball landed in front of the batsman's feet. The batsman bent down and picked the ball up to give it the keeper, who immediately appealed for 'obstruction'. Some of the fielders supported his appeal; others looked embarrassed and turned the other way. The batsman looked dumbfounded and there were shouts of "No" and "Never" from the pavilion. Everyone watched James to see what he would do. He didn't raise his finger. Instead he walked across to the other umpire and called the fielding captain to them. As other fielders started to join them he sent them away.

Then he spoke to the captain and the other umpire: 'The appeal is for obstruction. The laws of cricket say that a player can be dismissed for obstructing the field if in doing so he impedes a fielder while the ball is in play. To all intents and purposes the ball was dead, but I had not called it so. I don't think any advantage was gained by the batsman by his action, so I cannot give him out for obstruction. As there has been an appeal, I have also to consider whether he should be dismissed for 'handling the ball', which he clearly did. I think such a dismissal would normally only be given if the batsman handled the ball to stop it bouncing back on to his stumps after he had played it or if he stopped a fielder catching it. Again, I don't think the batsman's action on this occasion interfered with the passage of play. Much more important,' – here he looked at the captain – 'this is a friendly match and a fixture of long standing. If the batsman is given out, do you not think there is a chance of the relationship between the teams being soured? Would you like to withdraw the appeal?'

'I agree with you and I will withdraw the appeal,' said the captain.

'Thank you,' replied James. 'I will leave you to explain the nature of the decision, but before the game continues I want a word with the batsman and the keeper.' When they were brought to him, James said to them, 'The appeal has been withdrawn. The ball had been returned to the keeper; if he had caught it, it would be regarded as a dead ball – that is, it is no longer in play. However,' he said, looking directly at the batsman, 'the batsman may only pick up the ball in that situation if he has first obtained the keeper's permission to do so. Now, I suggest you two shake hands and we'll have a two-minute break while I explain the situation to the scorers.'

While he had a word with the scorers he noticed some strange activity amongst the parked cars. Seeing a paper bag blowing about on the far side of the field, he went over to pick it up and put it in his pocket, at the same time having a better look at the activity he had noticed.

When play was resumed, the batsman defended the first ball, but on the second ball he advanced down the pitch, swung at the ball, failed to make contact and was stumped. The score became

129 for six. There were no further incidents. Two more wickets fell before the score reached 157, giving the visitors a win by two wickets.

Hands were shaken, and players and umpires returned to the pavilion. Both the cars that had attracted James's attention had left independently before the close of play, and James, having handed in his borrowed umpire's coat, rejoined Ben and Mark. Mark had news of the injured umpire. After checks at the hospital he had been allowed home, with instructions to take things quietly for a couple of days and to dial 999 if he had any adverse reactions.

Many of the players, including both captains and the batsman and the wicketkeeper involved in the 'obstruction' incident, approached James and thanked him warmly for being a superb substitute umpire.

On the way home Ben and Mark wanted to know what he had said to the mother and how he had resolved the controversial appeal. James had just finished telling them when they had to stop because the road was blocked by two police cars. A female police officer came up to the car and told Mark that a car had left the road and it might be blocked for some time and they would be advised to seek another route. When Mark said he was an off-duty paramedic he was immediately welcomed as the driver was still trapped in the car, which was on its side with the front smashed into a tree. The ambulance had not yet arrived. After Mark had gone to see what help he could give, Ben and James got out of the car to look at the scene and enjoy some fresh evening air. It was then that James saw the crashed vehicle. It was one of the cars he had noticed at the match. He also recognised the female police officer. He had to cudgel his memory for a while before he remembered her name. Having done so, he approached her.

'It is Sergeant Cartwright, isn't it?'

She turned and looked at him, and she recognised him immediately and exclaimed, 'Mr Willoughby, what are you doing here?'

'I am one of the paramedic's passengers. We were just returning from watching a cricket match. I think I recognise the crashed car. It's a blue Peugeot, isn't it? I noticed it at the match we

27

have just come from. There was some strange activity going on between that car and a green Vauxhall Corsa – it looked as though something was being exchanged at the back of the cars. A reflection of the sun on the windows of another vehicle enabled me to see what looked like some plastic bags and some scales being used. Might this driver have been under the influence of drugs?'

While speaking he had been facing the sun, now lower in the sky, and he felt he was about to sneeze. He put a hand in his pocket for a handkerchief and discovered the bag he had picked up earlier. As he held it he noticed a strange smell. He passed the bag to the Sergeant and explained how he had come by it.

'Mr Willoughby, I wonder if you have been in the right place at the right time again. I think it has contained cannabis resin. Now, I wonder if you can give me any other information about the green Corsa?' She said this with a conspiratorial grin.

'Indeed, I think I can help. How about an 08 plate and the letters AEG?'

'Now, how did you remember that?'

'Easy, they are the first, fifth and seventh letters, which give 157. That was the number of runs needed to win the match, and the match was won for the loss of eight wickets.'

'Well, thanks – that's great. We'll send an alert out. I'm sure a crew somewhere will spot that car and have a "friendly" word with the occupants.'

'Jim,' said Ben, 'did you say that the letters were AEG, because I saw that car arrive during the tea interval when I went for a walk round the ground. I only saw the back as the driver drove past several places where he could park as though he was looking for someone. I thought the letters were AEC – that's what many of the London buses used to have on their radiators. Did you just see the front number plate?' Realising the Sergeant was also listening, he went on: 'Do you think they could be false plates and the person who made them up didn't make them identical?'

'It's possible,' said Sergeant Cartwright. 'Jim, what sort of activity did you see that caught your interest?'

'The activity was by the blue car. Two men were bending down and looking under the car and reaching just behind the nearside rear wheel. I don't think the petrol tank is on that side.'

'We will have a look as soon as we can. It shouldn't be too difficult as the car is lying on the driver's side, but as the ambulance team is now on the scene we shall have to wait until they have finished. It seems our paramedic is coming back to us.'

'Well, the driver is alive and conscious, if he can be so described. He is as high as a kite, probably from cocaine. I think he has a broken leg and possibly some internal injuries or broken ribs. He wasn't wearing his seat belt, but he was saved by the airbag, which will have given him some bruising. The ambulance crew will see to him, but they may need help from the fire brigade to get him out.'

'Thank you for your help,' said the Sergeant, who had been joined by another officer. 'Was there anyone else in the car?'

'Not now,' said Mark.

James then made another contribution: 'Shortly before we reached the accident I spotted someone walking, or rather staggering, towards us. I looked back after we had passed him and I saw him sit down by the side of the road. I wonder if he came from the car and if he is still around and injured.'

'Good point,' said Sergeant Cartwright. And turning to the other officer: 'What do you think, Robbo?'

'A dog car has just arrived, Jane. I'll get the dog and his handler to have a walk up the road.'

When he returned, Sergeant Cartwright introduced him to James and Ben: 'This is DC Robinson.' Then to the officer: 'James and Ben saw some unusual activity earlier at the back of the crashed car. We need to investigate behind the nearside rear wheel when we can, which should be fairly easy as the car is on its side. The car was in company with another, of which we have details thanks to Mr Willoughby and his friend. We have an alert out for the other car.'

'Mr Willoughby! You are the gentleman that tipped us off about the sheep and deer stealers, aren't you? I think we should recruit you as a part-time detective – don't you agree, Jane?'

Before Jane Cartwright could reply, Ben said to James, 'So you are the elderly resident who saw the van. I did wonder who it was, but you never said anything.'

The driver was released from the crashed car and taken by ambulance to hospital accompanied by a police officer. The dog handler and dog returned with another male, looking far from well, and arrangements were made for him also to go to hospital. A low-loader arrived to take the car away for forensic examination; but before it was loaded, Sergeant Cartwright and DC Robinson examined the area behind the rear wheel and discovered what looked like a bolted on compartment with a lever by which it could be opened.

As they stood up they looked at James and Ben, smiled and shouted, 'Bingo! Just as you suspected. It will need some persuasion to open it as the impact has twisted the frame of the car, but we'll see to that when we get it to the pound.'

The Sergeant's phone rang, and after she had held a short conversation she reported, 'They have found the green Corsa with a significant quantity of drugs on board. Driver and passenger have been detained and are being brought in for questioning. The car has been seized.'

She then turned to James, Ben and Mark and said, 'Very many thanks for your assistance. You have done a great job. I hope the cricket match was as successful.'

Ben replied, 'The match contained some surprises: an umpire was injured and Mark had to attend to him and send him to A & E for observation, and Jim took over as umpire for the second half, during which he had to deal with a controversial incident.'

'James Willoughby, is there anything you can't do?' Sergeant Cartwright exclaimed. 'You are certainly a man of many talents. We'll maybe call for you when we get another difficult incident.'

Looking around, she said, 'The road will be open again shortly and I'll be in touch to let you know how we progress. Goodbye for now.'

THE DOG RESCUER

At 2.45 p.m. on Wednesday 10 August – the second Wednesday of the month – James Willoughby was sitting on a bench in the central square of the village of Compton St Philip, having just exchanged his library books at the mobile library that parked in the car park next to the Church of St Philip. He was enjoying the warm sunshine and watching the few shoppers, some of them probably holidaymakers, who hadn't completed their shopping in the morning. He thought he could indulge in a few minutes of idleness before walking back to his apartment.

His interest was aroused when he saw an elderly lady, probably more advanced in age than his own eighty-five years, pushing a wheelchair containing a man likely to be older than her. They came steadily on until they reached where he was sitting.

'Good afternoon,' said James. 'You have made valiant progress; are you going to have a rest now?'

'Thank you, but no, not just yet. I must go into the library first, but could I leave my husband here beside your bench? He is only allowed a little exercise each day as he had a heart bypass operation last week, and stairs and the steps up into the library van are certainly out of bounds.'

'I shall look forward to his company, so take as long as you need. It wasn't very busy when I went in.'

'Thank you,' said her husband. 'Don't worry, Marjorie – I shall be quite all right here. See if you can find another Agatha Christie.'

The two men chatted about the weather, the pleasantness of their surroundings, the range of shops in the village and the prospects of the English cricket team due to start a Test match the next day.

When Marjorie returned, she sat down on the bench and said, 'I hope I wasn't too long, but I found you a murder mystery to solve, Roger. I hope he has behaved himself and not talked about politics, Mr, er . . .'

'Willoughby – James Willoughby. Now, your husband has been very well behaved – we have talked politics, the politics of English cricket. Is he good at solving murder mysteries?'

'Oh yes. Well, he thinks he is. He always finds a list of suspects and occasionally he gets it right – after he has found that all the others have alibis.' Without a breath, she continued: 'We are Roger and Marjorie Webster. Do you live in the village, Mr Willoughby?'

'Just outside the village at Cloverhill Court in Cloverfield Road. I have been there about six months.'

'Oh, I know where that is. Our home is in that direction, but only about half the distance. We live in Waterfall Close – do you know it?'

Roger eventually managed to get a word in: 'Do you answer to James or Jim, Mr Willoughby?'

'Both. There's a rather di—, sorry, a rather pleasant police lady I have met a couple of times recently and she has used all three forms of address to me.'

'We had better be getting back,' said Marjorie. 'I must make sure Roger doesn't get overtired.'

'I am concerned about you getting tired, Mrs Webster. Would you like me to take a turn as helmsman?'

'I really would appreciate that if you think you could manage. And call me Marjorie. I did find the outward journey a bit hard. I haven't pushed him so far before; but it will be another two weeks before the library comes again, by which time Roger might be walking.'

James had pushed Roger as far as the end of their close when Marjorie invited him to join them for a cup of tea. He declined, but said that he would be willing to take Roger for a 'walk' in his wheelchair on another occasion if that would be helpful. After a short debate, it was agreed that James would take Roger out two days later and they would follow the tarmac footpath that went out of the end of the close and on to a paved country footpath.

When he arrived at Roger and Marjorie's chalet bungalow, just before ten o'clock on Friday morning, James was asked if he had seen the short story that Marjorie had picked up in the library. It was called *Partly Old*.

'It is about James Willoughby helping the police to catch some animal rustlers,' said Marjorie. 'Have you seen it and is it about you?'

She showed him her copy.

'No, I don't think I have seen this. You say you found it in the library. I didn't notice it. It probably is about me, but I wonder who wrote it. How extraordinary! It's quite nicely presented, isn't it? I shall have to read it. I wonder why it has that title.'

'You can borrow this copy if you like. We have both read it.'

James and Roger made steady progress to the end of Waterfall Close, but had to stop briefly on two occasions as neighbours wanted to check on Roger's recovery. Eventually they reached the little passageway between two properties that gave access to the country footpath. They talked about the neighbours they had met, and Roger said they enjoyed really good support from the other occupants of the eight dwellings in the close. Then they discussed the first day's play in the Test Match and pondered whether England had made a strong enough start to be able to set a competitive total.

James asked, 'Have you made a start on the murder mystery Marjorie chose for you? She found an Agatha Christie novel, didn't she?'

'Yes, she found a Miss Marple story. A body appeared in the first chapter, and after about sixty pages we already have six suspects.'

'It sounds as though you are going to have your work cut out to solve that one. Miss Marple spends much of her time sitting knitting while she watches, listens and sifts thoughts in her mind. That should suit you while you are required to take things easy. Now, if your detective had been Hercules Poirot you might have had to be more energetic, especially if Chief Inspector Japp was striding about the place or Captain Hastings jumping to wrong conclusions or occasionally coming up with vital information without realising its relevance. It would be enough to wear you out. Let's hope your sleuthing can be confined to the written page today.'

'Agreed, James – we'll hope for a peaceful trip enjoying the sights and sounds of the countryside. Do stop and take a rest whenever you need to. There is usually something to observe and we can forget about murders although I did once see a sparrowhawk catch a small bird in the field to our right.'

To the right of the path, behind a hawthorn hedge, was a field where the grass had recently been cut, probably for sileage, and on the left there was a wood with no form of fencing. There didn't appear to be any paths going into the wood, and it looked as though the land fell away some six or eight metres from the path. The only tracks were probably made by small animals – possibly rabbits, foxes or stoats. Most of the trees were deciduous, and there was sufficient light near the path for the undergrowth to establish itself with a few young hawthorn bushes and brambles near the path. The cow parsley that skirted the hawthorn hedge was no longer in flower and it looked as though the farmer had cut most of it back, which had allowed some of the later small flowers to bloom. This was clearly a place for chalk-loving species, and James was delighted to see patches of delicate harebells creating a blue haze against the green background of the grass.

Roger pointed out a piece of cloth caught on some brambles and one or two strands of sheep's wool attached to the hedge, but there were no sheep in the field yet. Maybe they would be brought in when all the hay crop had been gathered. They had stopped to think about the way in which the fields were used when they heard a whimpering.

By then they had travelled about 150 metres along the path, and the gate by which they had entered was out of sight. Behind them, however, was a dog alone – a black cocker spaniel. As they looked at it, the dog ran towards them and then turned back and went a couple of feet into the wood and then came back, whimpering again. Again it came towards them, and then turned back again and repeated its part entry into the wood.

James had turned the wheelchair round so that Roger could see the dog.

'He seems in distress' said Roger.

'Certainly strange behaviour,' said James. 'I think he might be trying to tell us something. I'll see if I can find out if anything is the matter.'

Having made sure the wheelchair brake was on, he took a few steps towards the dog, who immediately came to him.

James stopped and bent down to talk to him: 'Is something the matter, boy? Do you need help?'

The spaniel barked, wagged his tail and ran off a few paces, and then looked round for James. Then he came back again, grabbed at James's trouser leg and tried to pull him.

'He obviously wants me to go with him,' said James. 'Will you be all right if I leave you here? I think there is something in the wood that is bothering him.'

'Yes, you go. I have my phone if we need to summon help. See what you can find out.'

James followed the dog, who ran ahead, then turned to check James was following, then ran on, again turning to check he was being followed. In this way they went several metres through the undergrowth and then James noticed a woman's shoe, then another, then clothing and then the naked body of a young woman. By now the dog was whimpering again and running round the body in distress, and when James looked into the dog's eyes it was clear that the dog was appealing to him to help.

He went over to the body, which appeared to be quite still. She was lying on her back, with bruising on her neck and eyes closed. He felt the girl's arms – she appeared no more than about eighteen – and felt some warmth, although initially he didn't think she was breathing. Nevertheless, he felt her neck to see if he could feel a pulse, and when he detected a slight movement he knew he had to work fast. He was wearing a light jacket, which he had put on, because there was a cool breeze when he left home.

He took this jacket off and placed it over the girl, then turned to the dog and cried, 'We've got to get help. Come on.'

Making as quick progress as he could, he yelled to Roger, 'Phone 999 for police, ambulance, possibly air ambulance as well. We may just be in time – there is a girl in there near to death.'

While Roger phoned and provided their location, James bent down to the dog: 'Well done, lad. We'll have some help here in a few minutes and we'll do our best to see she is all right. You have been very, very clever.'

He patted the dog and stroked him, and was rewarded by some almost joyful tail wagging.

Roger had done a good job with his phone call, giving clear information about their location, and with prompts from James, like 'clever dog', 'naked', 'about eighteen', 'weak pulse' and 'possible sexual attack', provided a clear picture of the situation. Within six minutes they heard sirens and, incredibly, four minutes later they heard the sound of a helicopter.

The ambulance team and the police arrived at almost the same time. James met them and took them immediately to the casualty, where the paramedics took over. They checked and found the faint pulse and prepared the girl to be carried on a stretcher to the air ambulance, which had been able to land in the field beyond the hedge. With drips and oxygen and all the paraphernalia needed to keep her alive, she was soon on her way to the hospital.

While the girl was being attended to on the ground, police officers started examining the scene and James looked around. He saw more of the girl's clothes and the dog's lead. He drew the attention of one of the police officers to the lead: he wondered if the girl had been able to free the dog from his lead so that he might seek help. If this was the case, the dog had not gone far, but rather wanted to stay near the girl.

When another police officer arrived, James recognised him as DC Robinson, whom he had met at the scene of a traffic accident about five weeks previously.

DC Robinson did a quick double take and exclaimed, 'Well, hello, Mr Willoughby! Incidents do seem to follow you around, or rather you stumble on them. I don't suppose you can keep up your record of being able to give us a car number.'

'I doubt it, but as I was walking towards Waterfall Close just after a quarter to ten a white BMW went past on its way out of the village at what I thought was excessive speed. I only saw the letters SPD, which I thought appropriate for a car at speed.'

'I'll make a note of that. You never know, it might have some bearing on the assault on this girl, which I hope will only turn out to be *attempted* murder.'

'Do you think you will need the dog's lead for forensics, or should I use it to take the dog home if we can find out where he belongs?'

'Yes, we do need to look after the dog, although he seems to have attached himself to you and will probably follow you wherever you go. Has he got a collar with a name or any ID on it?'

James bent down, stroking the spaniel, who seemed delighted to be the centre of attention, while he felt and found a collar and a name tag without a name, but with a number and a postcode. James read out the details and said that it was a local postcode. DC Robinson called his office to see if they could identify the postcode. He was given the name of the road and was also told that they had just received a phone call from a worried lady who said that her daughter, Melanie Hardy, and her dog had not returned home when they were expected. She had heard the sirens and put two and two together. On this occasion DC Robinson thought that her two and two didn't make five. James thought he recognised the name of the road, but wasn't certain of its location. However, when he mentioned it to Roger he knew where it was. He also suggested that Roger should phone Marjorie to let her know that they were all right and the police and ambulance had not been called for them.

DC Robinson agreed that James and Roger should take the dog to its home, with a police constable to give the worried mother more details. In the meantime the 'scene of crime' team would search for more evidence in the wood. James remembered that Roger had spotted what appeared to be a piece of cloth on some brambles. When they found the place, the police looked at the cloth and realised that it was a woolly hat. The ground around it seemed disturbed, as though a struggle had taken place there, during which the hat may have been lost. The hat, which had some black hairs attached to it, was placed carefully inside an evidence bag for forensic analysis later. As the girl had fair hair, the police considered that this could provide an important lead to finding the attacker.

James, Roger and the police constable made their way to the address provided by the dog's collar tag with James looking after the dog and the Constable pushing Roger, who guided them to Melanie's home. Mrs Hardy saw them coming and met them on the doorstep wringing her hands, agitated and fearful as to what she was going to hear.

James tried to calm her: 'Mrs Hardy, I am James Willoughby. My friend Roger and I were stopped in our walk by this very clever dog, who asked, in his way, for help. We don't know his name.'

'Pepper', said Mrs Hardy.

Hearing his name, the dog jumped up and wagged his tail.

James continued: 'I followed Pepper into the wood, where I found Melanie. It looked as though she had been attacked. She was unconscious. Roger, here, immediately rang 999 and the emergency services, including the air ambulance you probably heard, arrived within ten minutes. With the helicopter it was possible to take her quickly to hospital for a proper assessment of her condition and treatment. Melanie was far enough into the wood for us not to see her from the path, and if it had not been for Pepper we would not have known she was there. PC Porter, here, will give you more details as to where Melanie has been taken, and he will want to ask you some questions about your daughter and if you have any idea of people who might have attacked her this morning.'

While they were talking, a message came through to PC Porter to say that Melanie had regained consciousness and her condition was being stabilised. She was going to be kept in hospital for a few days under observation. Mrs Hardy seemed a little reassured by the news, but wanted to know where her daughter was and if she could go and see her.

Leaving Pepper with Mrs Hardy, James and Roger left PC Porter to ask his questions and make arrangements for Mrs Hardy to go to the hospital. But before they parted from the Constable, he asked them to keep their ears open for any information about strange cars or vans that had been in the area earlier in the morning. In response to a question from Roger he also gave them a number to phone if they had anything to report. He also asked Mrs Hardy when Melanie had left home with the dog, and was told about eight-thirty.

As the Hardy's home was on the other side of the village from their own homes, James and Roger had to pass through the centre of the village. It was while they were crossing the village square and passing the cars parked there that they met James's friend Ben Foster.

Ben had just come out of the village store and post office, and James was surprised to see him shopping so late in the morning; so he said as much: 'Hello, Ben. You're shopping late today. You are usually one of the early birds.'

Then he introduced Roger and Ben to each other before Ben replied, 'I don't know, Jim. I must be getting old. This is my second visit today. I had just finished getting a few things, but still had to call at the post office to send a letter by recorded delivery. When I got here I collided with a young man in a hurry. He just called a quick "Sorry, mate" and ran on. I watched him. He suddenly stopped, felt his head, then looked back the way he had just come. He felt his head again, as though he had lost his hat, then got into a car and drove off at great speed.'

'Was it a white BMW by any chance?' asked James.

'Yes, it was. I got a good look at it and did your trick and tried to get the number, but he was so quick I only got part of it. The first two letters were too dirty to read, but it went on 02 S something.'

'Well done, Ben. That sound's like it, doesn't it, Roger. I can add the other two letters – PD. There was a nasty attack on a young girl earlier this morning – you may have heard the police and ambulance sirens and the air ambulance. We found her at about ten fifteen – your man may have been the attacker, especially as a woolly hat was found near the scene. Did you get a good look at him? We have a number to phone the police if we have further information.'

'Oh, yes, he was clearly agitated and that made me look at him. I think I could give a good description. I was so busy observing him that I completely forgot my letter, which is why I have had to come back again.'

James pondered. 'I wonder if there are any police nearby. How about trying that number, Roger?'

Roger got a response immediately. He explained that they thought they had some information and where they were, and was asked if they could wait and someone would be with them shortly. In less than five minutes a police car arrived. James introduced Ben and explained that he had been in the area at about nine forty-five and had probably seen the same car, as well as the man who drove away in it.

Ben then took up the story and described the suspect. The officer made a note, complimented Ben on his description and phoned the further details of the BMW in the hope that it could be traced. The policeman thought Ben's observation about the man appearing as though he might have just realised that he had lost a hat and that he had dark hair could provide an important clue. He expected that the hairs on the hat would be checked for DNA. He also said that the investigation of the area where the girl was found, and the girl herself, could provide additional clues. He thanked them again and said that he or one of his colleagues would be in touch again as the investigation progressed. As part of that investigation he said he was going to ask in the shops if anyone had seen the car and its driver. He hoped to find out what time it arrived.

James, Roger and Ben continued their journey, with Ben offering to take a turn at pushing. When they reached Waterfall Close, Ben continued on his way home for the second time that morning and Roger and James went to Roger's home to tell Marjorie about their exciting experience. Marjorie insisted on making coffee for everyone and then settled down to hear the account. They agreed that it must have been a terrible ordeal for the young girl and hoped she would make a full recovery and be able to continue with her life without severe mental scars. They also thought the dog, Pepper, should be recognised for his part in the rescue.

The three of them hoped that the police had sufficient evidence to be able to solve this near-murder mystery quickly.

Roger then remembered something one of the policemen said and asked James, 'What did that policeman mean when he recognised you and suggested you had a habit of stumbling on incidents and something about car numbers?' Before James could answer, he continued: 'In that story that Marjorie found in the library, you – if it is you in the story – spotted the number of the thieves' van. Is that what the policeman was referring to?'

'Very good, Detective Roger! You found the answer without knowing that five weeks ago the police apprehended some drug smugglers after I again noticed part of a car number. That incident was so recent that DC Robinson recognised me.'

'Do you think that incident will go into print as well? If it does we shall have to make sure we read it.'

'I don't know. I didn't know the rustlers' arrest would be written about and I haven't read it to check for accuracy. And I think, Roger, you have had more than enough excitement for one who is supposed to be recovering from surgery. Marjorie, I think you will have to keep him in sight. I won't offer to take him out for a few days, but I might call next Thursday after I have been to the market, unless we get any news before then.'

'Here is the book, James. Let us know what you think of it.'

'Many thanks. I am very curious to read it. I think I know what I shall be doing this afternoon.'

By this time, midday had passed, so James bade them goodbye and made his way home.

When he arrived at his apartment block he discovered a rather battered large brown envelope in his pigeonhole, marked 'Private and Confidential'. He took it upstairs with him, pondering what it could be, and noticed that it had been posted at the end of July, two weeks earlier. He wondered where it had been in that time – stuck in the bottom of a postbag or wandering around the country. He would have his lunch first and then examine his two curious items.

He warmed some soup and made himself a ham-and-lettuce sandwich, then sat down to read the story, thinking the battered envelope could wait a few minutes longer before being opened. He was fascinated by what he read. Most of the facts were accurate, except that his address had been slightly changed and the descriptions of what he might have been thinking matched his character very well. But who was the author, or was more than one person responsible for it?

Next he opened the envelope and discovered that it was from Sergeant Jane Cartwright, the police officer whom he had met on two occasions. With the letter was another copy of *Partly Old*. He was asked to read the story and let her know in a week if he had any objection to it being published. Sergeant Cartwright wrote that she had had some assistance in compiling the story from two of his grandchildren, and she hoped it might be a means to flushing out two collaborators of the thieves who were on police radar, but were still at large.

Well, it was a bit late now for him to object, but while he was thinking what the implications of its publication might be the phone rang. It was Sergeant Cartwright with a message from DC Robinson to say that the driver of the white BMW had been traced and arrested pending further enquiries. There was also news of Melanie: the hospital thought she would make a full recovery, but she might not have survived if she had lain in the wood undiscovered for another hour.

While she was on the phone, he asked her about his story, which he had just read and what impact the police thought it might have. He explained that he had only just become aware of it, so she arranged a date when she would come and talk to him about possible scenarios that might follow and tell him more about the information they already had.

Nearly four weeks later, when he was sitting on the bench outside the library, a cocker spaniel and its owner and her mother found him there. The dog greeted him with glee, wagging his tail and jumping up on the bench to sit beside him. When the dog had quietened down, Melanie and her mother thanked him profusely for helping her. This was Melanie's first day out since coming home from hospital. When James looked at her he realised what a beautiful girl she was – so vibrant, and altogether different from the near-corpse that Pepper, the dog, and he had rescued.

The following February Melanie's attacker was convicted of sexual assault and attempted murder, and seven further sexual assaults on other girls, and sentenced to twenty years in prison.

REVENGE IS NOT ALWAYS SWEET

By the middle of September summer was drawing to a close and in a week's time the autumn equinox would have arrived. Although the meteorologists had said the autumn had already begun, James Willoughby, having lived through eighty-five summers, preferred to stick to the seasons determined by the passage of the sun rather than dates that fitted neatly into the calendar. Therefore, on the morning of Saturday 18 September he was to be found sitting on a bench in the square of Compton St Philip enjoying some late summer sun having shopped for the few items he needed. To passers-by he might have appeared to be dozing, but he was quite alert and responded immediately to a cheerful 'hello' from a lovely young lady.

The young lady was Melanie Hardy, whom he had rescued, with the help of her dog, after a vicious sexual attack five weeks earlier. If he and her dog had not acted so swiftly she would have died.

'Good morning, dear. How are you? Have you nearly fully recovered from your ordeal? And where is my little canine friend Pepper?'

'I have had to leave Pepper at home. He was scampering madly around the garden when he trod on a sharp thorn on a rose cutting that Dad had missed when he was doing some tidying-up. We managed to get the thorn out, but it is still sore. We put some cream on it given us by the vet, but he has to rest it for a day or two. Trying to get Pepper to rest is not easy, I can tell you.'

'Have you much shopping to do or could you spare a few minutes to have a coffee with an old man?'

'I'd love to. I only came down for a paper, mainly to see if I felt capable of going for a walk on my own. It will be like having morning coffee with a surrogate grandad.'

Melanie fetched her paper from the shop next door to the baker's. At the back of the baker's there was a little coffee-bar area.

When their coffees and biscuits had been served James remarked, 'You appear to have made a wonderful recovery. Are you fully healed physically, and what about psychological scars? I doubt if you have been near that wood again.'

'I am still a little sore in places, but nearly all the bruising has gone and I can breathe properly now. I am not sure about going down that path again – certainly not on my own. Have you been there since?'

'No, I haven't; it's a pity because I was enjoying that walk. I keep thinking I will venture that way while the weather is still pleasantly warm. If you feel you wish to try to lay a demon to rest, perhaps we could take a walk there together.'

'That's a lovely idea, but I can only go at the weekend as I am returning to school on Monday. I have missed a few days already, and A levels will come round quickly. I am a little apprehensive about Monday as I think my friends will want all the details.'

'Melanie, my dear, if I may offer some advice, I suggest that if you think it will help you to talk about it then tell them. It may be cathartic. But if you feel you are not ready, just tell them it was a horrible experience and rather than reliving it by talking about it, you would prefer to fill your mind with other matters. I am sure they will understand, particularly if they are friends worth having. Now, tell me what subjects you are studying for A level and what other interests you have.'

'Thank you for that advice. My A-level subjects are English, history and mathematics. I also completed a one-year course in biology. I'm not sure what I want to study if I go to university, or indeed what career I want to pursue. I am trying to keep options open. I also liked music and religious studies before I joined the sixth form.'

'Do you play any musical instruments or sing?'

'Yes, I have passed Grade 5 in both piano and cello. I play the piano now mainly for pleasure, but I play the cello in the school orchestra. I used to sing in the church choir, but I fell out with the choir-mistress. I think I might rejoin now that they have a new organist.'

'If you rejoin the choir I shall look out for you on a Sunday. I'm afraid my choir singing days are over, but it sounds as if you lead quite a busy life. Any sporting prowess?'

'Well, last term the girls were allowed to play cricket and we played two matches, winning one and drawing the other. I did quite well in that as I had played with my two older brothers, so I had developed some skill, although . . .'

'They wanted you to field while they batted and bowled?' suggested James.

'Absolutely! How did you guess? But they soon realised that if they didn't allow me to take a full part I wouldn't play, and my dad backed me up.'

'How old are your brothers?'

'Tom is twenty-two and at Exeter Uni, while Luke is twenty and at Bristol. Another week and then their terms start. They both played cricket for the village team during the vac. The club only has a men's team, although there is talk about starting a ladies' team next year and there may be winter nets. I shall go to those if they manage to get them organised.'

'It's possible I may have met your brothers, because I was asked to substitute for an umpire who was injured during a friendly match.'

'Oh, it was you! I didn't go to that match, but my brothers told me about it. Didn't you have to deal with a controversial situation? They were full of praise for the way you handled it.'

'Thank you.' They finished their coffees and James said. 'It's been lovely chatting with you, Melanie. I hope we have not been too long. Do you think you had better phone your parents to let them know you are all right, but have been talking to an old bore – or, if you prefer, a friend?'

'Not an old bore, Mr Willoughby – a friend, yes.'

'You needn't call me Mr Willoughby. It's a bit of a mouthful.

Call me James or Jim. And it might help to make the difference in our ages feel a bit less.'

'I'm not sure about that, but may I call you SG? That stands for Surrogate Grandad. Both my grandfathers died before I was three, and you aren't all that old, are you?'

'That sounds a grand idea. As to being old, somewhere recently I was described as 'partly old'. Time to go, I think.'

'Can we meet next Saturday and, if the weather is OK, go for that walk?'

'Sure, Melanie. Meet by the bench at ten thirty? Perhaps Pepper will be recovered so that he can come with us. Here's a card with my phone number if you can't manage it.'

'Great, SG! See you then. I'll phone you in any case and give you my number. Bye,' she trilled, and was gone.

'Well,' thought James, 'that girl seems to have made a remarkable recovery. I hope her youth and resilience will help her to avoid a delayed reaction to her ordeal, particularly when the case against her attacker comes to court. I'd like to keep in touch with her so that I can give her support if she needs it – as much, that is, as an old man can give. Perhaps encouragement is the key.'

While he had been thinking, he had been making his way home and didn't immediately notice Marjorie and Roger Webster walking towards him; but when he looked up he recognised them.

'Good morning,' called James as they got nearer. 'You're walking well, Roger. Have you been able to dispense with the wheelchair?'

'That's right,' said Marjorie before Roger could get his breath for a reply. 'The consultant is very pleased with his progress and I don't have to push him any longer. How are you, James?'

'Very well, thank you. I have just spent a pleasant half an hour with Melanie – the young girl we rescued. She seems to be making a very good recovery and will be going back to school to resume her A-level courses on Monday.'

'That's really good news,' said Roger. 'With the attacker in custody until his trial, it's a much better outcome than we feared at one time.'

They bade each other goodbye, and James continued on his

way, this time trying to remember if he had decided what to have for lunch and, if he had, what it was. He was nearly home, passing the park with its small lake, when he was reminded that he had a fishcake in the fridge, and that he was planning to cook a couple of new potatoes to go with it and a green salad.

The following week was pleasantly warm, but on Friday it rained most of the day and the following day was expected to bring in a wet start to autumn. In the evening Melanie phoned and it didn't take long for them to postpone their walk for a week.

Melanie went on to tell him, 'When I arrived home last Saturday humming, Mum and Dad wanted to know how I felt about walking on my own and who I had had coffee with, so I said I had had a lovely chat with SG. "Who is SG?" they wanted to know, so I told them and that we had planned to go for a walk together as a further step in my recuperation. They hoped it wouldn't be too tiring for an old man – no, they said an "elderly gentleman" – so I said, "SG is only partly old." Dad pricked up his ears at that and said that he had been sent a short story called *Partly Old* by the police, and it is about someone called James Willoughby. He was sent it because he runs a security firm and may be called to provide protection. Is that you and are you in danger?'

'Oh dear,' thought James, 'I had better tell her.'

Then he answered her: 'Melanie, you are not to worry about me. If you read the story, which has got my name in it, you will see that I played a small part in the arrest of some criminals. The police think there could possibly be some repercussions, so they are making sure that none of us is taken by surprise. They may even be able to catch other members of the gang. Don't say anything to anyone else and I'll tell you more when we go for our walk next week. Sleep well tonight and have sweet dreams.'

After he had put the phone down, he admonished himself: 'James, you are getting forgetful – you never asked her about her week back at school.'

The following Saturday was bright and sunny. Several of the trees had started to turn rich autumn colours, although a few had lost leaves during the wind and rain of the previous weekend. As the daylight each day was getting less and the temperatures cooler, James decided to wear a quilted anorak and a cap. Next week it would be October and he would have to look out his gloves and perhaps a scarf.

Arriving at the bench, he had not had time to sit down when a car pulled up and out got Melanie with her dog. When Pepper had finished his excited greeting, Melanie introduced James to her father.

'I am very pleased to meet you, Mr Willoughby. I am Stuart Hardy. My wife and I would be pleased if you would come back to our home with Melanie for coffee after your walk.'

'That's very kind. I don't think we shall be more than an hour.'

Melanie, James and Pepper set off, with the cocker spaniel keen to get going.

James asked, 'Well, my girl, how has the past fortnight been for you, particularly at school?'

'Oh, OK. I took your advice and deflected questions about my ordeal, but later I was able to give some info to my closest friends. It's been all right. I gather the teachers have been given some details, but they have not probed and we are well into term now.'

It didn't take many minutes for them to leave the houses behind, and shortly afterwards they came to the gate that led to the footpath that made its way between the wood and the hedge next to the field. It was along this path that Melanie had been attacked, dragged into the wood, raped and strangled until she lost consciousness. Pepper had stayed with her until James and his friend Roger came along the path three-quarters of an hour later. The dog had alerted them and almost dragged James into the wood to rescue his mistress.

They passed through the gate, and after a few yards James stopped and made Melanie look around her.

'Now just look at those trees, Mel. Look at all those different colours. Some leaves are already turning orange and red, and before long we shall see the golden yellow of the field maples. There are many different species here, with quite a few silver birches. In about three weeks it will be a splendid kaleidoscope of colour, especially on a sunny day.'

'It's beautiful,' responded Melanie. 'And look – there are sheep in the field. We must keep Pepper on the lead, although I don't think he would be able to get through the hedge.'

They continued walking, and then James spoke: 'In August, along this part of the path there were harebells flowering near the hedge. Do you know what harebells look like?'

'I'm not sure. Are they blue, like bluebells?'

'They are blue, but smaller and much more delicate and a lighter blue. When we saw them they showed up well against the green of the grass through which they were growing. They like a chalky soil. It's many years since I last saw some, so I shall have to remember to look for them next summer. Just look how many sheep there are in that field. It certainly is a large flock and they all look quite content, don't they?'

While they walked she had linked her arm though his and looked at the things he pointed out to her. In this way they passed the spot where she had been dragged from the path, and they continued in a companionable silence for a few minutes before he spoke again: 'How are you feeling, Melanie?'

'I am fine, thank you. I like walking with you, SG. Have we passed the . . . ?'

'We passed the place of your ordeal about six minutes ago and nothing nasty happened.'

'Oh, I didn't notice and I don't think Pepper did. Thank you for guiding me past it.'

'Pepper knew where we were. He stopped slightly, smelled the air and looked up at you and then carried on. His paw doesn't seem to be bothering him, does it? If we carry on along this path, can we get back to the village?'

'Yes, we can. The path will turn to the right soon, and a bit later there is another path off to the right which will bring us eventually to Coltsford Road. Its only about seven or eight minutes to home from there.' She paused for a few seconds and then said, 'I have read the story *Partly Old*. Is it all true or just a story? And if it is true, does the fact they have sent Dad a copy mean you are in danger?'

'Now, you have asked several questions there. Just as the man in the story is partly old, so the story is partly true. I am not sure how it came about, but I think it was a combined effort of the police sergeant and two of my granddaughters after they met at the stables where they all have horses. I believe one of the criminals was overheard making a threat that they would get their revenge against the person who tipped off the police which led to their arrest. The three who were caught have been detained until their trial, but there may be other members of the gang who will try to exact that revenge. Although some of the story is accurate, some is not. You might think that I have been set up as a decoy, but I have protection. This little button in my lapel is a tracking device so the police – and possibly, by now, your dad – know where I am. Satisfied?'

'Yes, but I hope no one will try to hurt you. Please be careful. How many grandkids have you got?'

'Five – three girls and two boys. My son has two girls, Carole and Lucy, and one boy, Robin, and my daughter has a boy, Phil, and a girl, Holly. Their ages range from twenty-nine to twenty, and three have birthdays near Christmas. You can probably work out which were the Christmas babies.' Then he added, with a smile, 'I also have a surrogate granddaughter.'

'That's me, yes? Do you think I could meet them and see the horses?'

'I think that might be arranged. I'll see what we can do.'

By now Pepper had started to pull on his lead, because they were nearly home.

James was warmly welcomed by Melanie's parents, and the four of them were soon sitting down with warm mugs of coffee. Stuart and Becky Hardy asked how the walk had gone, and Melanie immediately responded by saying that she felt no concern or apprehension when they passed the place where she had been assaulted. In fact, she explained that SG had been busy talking to her and showing her things and they had passed the spot without her knowing where it was. She said she had felt quite safe all the time; but when SG had answered her question about issues around the *Partly Old* story, she felt worried about his safety.

Before Stuart could say a word, James told Melanie that her dad had probably been monitoring their progress all the time. Melanie asked her dad if that was true.

He replied, 'I looked for and saw the button in Mr Willoughby's lapel, and he knew that I had seen it. We didn't need to say anything.'

The two men smiled at each other as though they knew things of which mother and daughter were ignorant.

Becky Hardy asked, 'Have you two been in touch with each other before?'

'Yes and no,' said James. 'Let us say that we both have access to the same information, and perhaps our contact has been through telepathy rather than telephony.'

'I think, though', said Stuart, 'perhaps we do need to have a chat about procedures if they become necessary. Shall I give you a lift home? We can talk on the way.'

'Can I come, Dad?' asked Melanie.

'There are matters your SG and I need to discuss that need not concern you, and you could be really helpful to your mother getting lunch ready. I think you are a very lucky girl to have a champion like James.'

'I know,' replied Melanie. 'Thank you, dear SG.' And she skipped across the room and placed a kiss on his cheek.

'You have my number – you can always phone me if you want to have a chat. Work hard at school next week. Let me know if you rejoin the church choir.' Then he turned to Becky Hardy and said, 'Thank you very much for the coffee. I think Mel is going to be all right. She seems to be making an amazing recovery.'

When they were in the car Stuart asked James if had his panic button with him. James confirmed that it was in his pocket. Stuart informed him that the panic button also contained a radio transmitter so that sounds (including voices) could be heard by the police and at his own security base. He went on to say, 'We have a new piece of kit which can be fixed to your headgear or placed in your lapel. It combines both a camera and a radio. Both means of communication can be received and recorded by those monitoring your movements. It sounds a bit invasive, but if you tap the device, the monitoring station will be alerted and, if necessary, help can be despatched immediately. We also have the facility of having covert observation located in your vicinity. I will bring you the equipment on Monday and show you how to use it.'

'That all sounds a bit like cloak-and-dagger stuff. I hope it brings the required result. When do you think someone might strike.'

'We don't expect any action for several days, but we need to be prepared. He, or they, will need to make enquiries and we hope to pick up that activity. We shall be checking CCTV installations in the area – including shops, pubs, eating places, the mobile library and newspaper offices. We shall be asking personnel in those places to inform us immediately if they are questioned about the location of Cloverhill Court or if they know of a Mr James Willoughby. Copies of *Partly Old* will also be visible in several outlets, and we shall want to know if anyone shows interest in it.'

'I see. Have you considered that someone might pose as a reporter and visit Sam Small at Bucklands Farm, perhaps with a story about wanting to talk to the person who is to be given an award for his quick thinking?'

'No, I don't think we have. That's a very valid point. I'll follow it up. I'll call with the kit on Monday morning – will ten o'clock be OK? Good. I'll see you then.'

On the following Wednesday evening Melanie phoned.

'SG, how are you?' she said. 'I want to ask you something. It's my eighteenth birthday on the 30th and Mum and Dad asked if I wanted a party, but I said I'd like to go out for a meal. Will you be one of my guests? It's a Saturday.' She named a place and a time and said transport would be arranged.

He gave the impression of consulting a busy engagement diary and then said, 'Melanie, my dear, I am greatly honoured to be invited and my diary says I can accept as I have no other engagements for that date. How lovely – a very special day!'

The copies of the story had been placed in the shops and most of the shopkeepers had read them, but no enquiries had been made that triggered an alert and James began to think that nothing would happen. When he went to the mobile library, on Wednesday 13 October, he saw a man sitting on 'his' bench reading *Partly Old*.

When he came out of the library, having changed his books,

the man spoke to him: 'Excuse me, mate – can you tell me where Cloverhill Court is?'

James pulled his anorak more tightly round him, touching the button in his lapel and said, 'Cloverhill Court, did you say? I can't think of anywhere with that name, although I haven't lived here many months. There is a Cloverfield Road.' And he gave the man some fairly vague directions. The man then walked across the square and got into a black Audi, and James made a note of the number as he drove off. He noticed that a few seconds later another car passed him and followed the Audi.

As he was walking home, a car drew up alongside him and he was relieved to see that Stuart was the driver.

'Would you like a lift?' Stuart called.

When they reached Cloverfield Court, they spotted the Audi parked further up the road. James noticed the man who had asked for directions walking along the road looking for names on the houses, some of which were quite large and set back from the road. He could see that there was another man sitting in the passenger seat of the car.

Stuart said, 'I'll come in with you to make sure you are safely home.'

On the way in, James noticed that the list of residents was incomplete and his name had been removed while a different name was against his apartment number. Obviously, one of Stuart's team had been busy.

'Stairs or lift?' asked Stuart.

'What do you advise?'

'If you can manage them, I suggest the stairs.'

They climbed the stairs and James realised how much he had appreciated his car ride as he found himself getting short of breath. When they reached his flat, Stuart asked him to check that nothing had been disturbed and then asked about his plans for the rest of the day and the next, suggesting he keep his surveillance device switched on night and day. As James's plan for the next day was a trip to the weekly market, Stuart wanted to know the time he would leave his apartment so that he could provide a 'tail' who would keep him in sight covertly.

James slept well, but woke with what he thought was a touch of indigestion. He decided on a small breakfast of cereals and a slice of toast. His other option was a boiled egg, but he remembered that he had used his last egg, so needed to get some from the market.

He made his purchases at the market and then, feeling a little tired, he sat down on a convenient seat for a rest before returning home. He had been there for only a minute when the man who asked him for directions to Cloverhill Court appeared in front of him with another man.

He immediately pressed the button in his pocket and then said as coolly as he could manage, 'Oh, good morning. Did you find the place you were looking for yesterday.'

'We think we have found what we were looking for. I think you are James Willoughby as we heard someone address you by that name. We aren't very happy with you as you interfered with our business in August by interrupting our supply chain.'

His voice had been gradually getting more menacing, but James tried to remain calm and asked, 'What business are you in and how did I inconvenience you?'

'We are wholesale meat suppliers to butchers, and a consignment did not reach us because you decided to interfere. It has harmed our business, and we think you should be harmed as well.'

'Right – I think I understand. You supply retailers, such as butchers' shops, and someone supplies you with animals or carcasses that have been bought at market. The animals previously have been reared at considerable cost of time and expense by farmers, who in their turn may have bought young animals at market. So you must be talking about a break in the supply chain where your suppliers, instead of buying, stole the animals. Whether you knew about it or not, you received stolen goods, which is, I believe, a criminal offence. And I suggest that you keep that knife in your pocket before you are seen to be carrying an offensive weapon, which is another indictable offence.'

'A pretty speech, my friend. You explain it so well, so it seems you knew what you were doing when you informed on us.'

'So you admit it was your organisation.'

'We have gone to considerable trouble to find you, and we are not going to be put off. I am just debating how we should teach you a lesson.'

They had been so busy threatening James they had not realised that four of the people behind them had not just been passing by. So they were surprised when their arms were suddenly pinned behind their backs and secured by handcuffs.

'Well done, Jim,' said DC Robinson. 'I think we have all that on video and it should be the evidence we need to dismantle this illegal operation.'

As the two men were led away to a couple of police vans, Stuart appeared. He took James back to his apartment, where Sergeant Jane Cartwright met them. After a debriefing session they left James to rest, which he did while sitting in his chair gazing at the countryside.

During the next few days both of his families visited and heard about his experience. Adam, his son, and Rachel had had an account from the Sergeant via their daughters, who had discussed the case while seeing to their horses; while his daughter, Ruth, with her husband, Michael Dawson, learned how the 'old geezer', as once Phil, their son, had unknowingly described his grandfather, had again helped the police with the arrest of criminals.

Late on Friday 29 October, Melanie answered the front doorbell and had a large bouquet of flowers thrust into her arms. The card simply said 'Happy 18th Birthday, Melanie. Much love, SG.'

Melanie took her time coming down to breakfast the next day, but was in time to hear her mother on the phone say, 'I am so sorry to hear that. He will be missed, but hopefully he will recover. Thank you for letting me know.'

'What was that about? asked Melanie.

'That was Rachel Willoughby, SG's daughter-in-law. I'm afraid SG won't be with us this evening. He had a heart attack during the night. He managed to call the emergency services and has been taken to hospital. His son is with him, and his daughter is on the way. He is conscious and sends you his love and hopes you will have a lovely day.'

Melanie clapped her hands over her face and said in a small voice, 'Oh no, he won't die, will he?'

THE CHOICE

At ten o'clock on a Friday morning in late June, Brian Mason was sitting on a park bench pondering his future – if, indeed, he had a future. He was thirty-four and had been married for five years. He had a job as a delivery driver, but by now he might be unemployed, not having clocked in this morning. He could not face the thought of going to work or of going home. How had he got to this state?

His childhood, as an only child, had been quite pleasant, although he saw little of his father, who was a long-distance lorry driver and could be away for two weeks at a time. He enjoyed his schoolwork and was making good progress until his mother died at the beginning of his GCSE year. As soon as his mother was buried, Brian's life changed. His father obtained employment locally and took over the running of the home and the control of Brian. Brian found that any freedom that he had enjoyed previously, to pursue his interests, was now seriously curtailed. He was required to keep the house clean, to provide his father's evening meals and to work in the garden at weekends. His phone was confiscated, his school trombone lessons were discontinued and the loaned instrument returned to the school. His school standards deteriorated, and at the end of the year his GCSE results were considerably lower than had been predicted a year earlier.

His hopes of a sixth-form education vanished when, as a sixteen-year-old, his father found him work as a bricklayer's mate with a construction firm. He was allowed to keep twenty-five per cent of his take-home pay, but was still expected to do his work in the house. Although he would have chosen a different career, he made good progress and learned a range of skills, including driving. His father was pleased he could drive as he could be called upon to provide a taxi service in his father's car for his father's nights out at the local pub.

By the time he was twenty-six he was earning good money as a delivery driver for a supermarket chain; and he was able to keep more than half his pay, which enabled him to save for the future. He was surprised when one of the girls at work expressed her affection for him. Two years later they were married, and within a year he discovered that her attraction for him was for his pay packet and his ability to look after their rented accommodation. While he looked after their flat, his wife went out partying two or three times a week.

As he sat on the bench he felt trapped. After reviewing his life for an hour he resolved to take action. He decided that he would 'run away'. He remembered that his wife was going to a hen party and would be away for the weekend. That would give him time to make his plans and disappear. He now had a sizeable sum in his bank account, of which his wife knew nothing, and he had yet to collect his wages.

He went to his place of work, apologised for being late, said he had had to deal with an emergency family crisis (he didn't explain that he was the crisis), handed in his resignation and collected the pay for his week's work, plus one week's holiday pay that was owing to him. Arriving home only just before his wife was due to leave, he gave her some cash and said he would give her the rest of his wages when she returned. He told her he hoped she would have a good weekend.

When she was gone he put a few items of clothing in a holdall together with his bank book and papers relating to it, found his birth certificate and driving licence and, with his inflated pay packet, left the flat. He planned to be at least 200 miles away before anyone knew he had disappeared.

He set out with an expectation worthy of Mr Micawber that something would turn up. He realised that the new requirement that passengers on public transport should wear face coverings assisted his escape, for with a cap as well he should not be too recognisable on CCTV cameras. Nevertheless, he made frequent changes between trains and buses and walked when he could not find a convenient connection. The nights were warm, and he slept for a while in a bus shelter during his second night, having walked most of the previous night.

On the Sunday morning he was walking along a country road when he noticed what appeared to be three farm cottages spaced out and set back from the road. He thought this might be a good place to rest, and discovered the first one had a notice in the window saying 'Room to Let – Apply Within'. He knocked on the door and it swung open. He called out, but he received no answer, so went in.

Through an open door he could see a man sitting in an armchair and a table at his side with part of a meal on it. He called again and knocked on the door, but received no response. As he investigated further he realised that the man was dead and had probably been so for two or three days. Brian was about to make a hasty retreat when he had an idea. The man looked quite like himself, so he decided to look around. An hour later he cycled away from the cottage as Ronald Reginald Brocklebank, having exchanged his driving licence and birth certificate. He had also acquired a passport and a significant quantity of cash. As far as he could tell, the only trace of Brian Mason's existence on this earth was the body in the cottage. The only mode of transport had been the bicycle: there was no sign of a car.

After cycling about forty miles he came to a garden centre on the outskirts of a town. As the tea room in the garden centre was still open in mid afternoon he stopped for some refreshment. On the table was a notice advertising situations vacant. They wanted a delivery driver who could also help around the centre. When the centre closed for the day the new Ron – the new employee – went in search of accommodation. He found the B & B to which his new boss had directed him, and he booked in for a week, thinking he might be able to find a place of his own in the next few days.

Six months later, happier than he had been for the last twenty years and living in his own rented flat, he returned one lunchtime after making deliveries and joined two of the other staff for a lunch break. As soon as he sat down, one of them showed him a newspaper with an item in the personal column seeking the whereabouts of Ronald Reginald Brocklebank and giving a phone number.

'Perhaps you've come into some money, Ron,' said his colleague.

After work, he used the smartphone he had bought himself to respond to the enquiry in the paper and agreed to meet a Mr Lewis at 6 p.m. in a local hotel the following day. He arrived just before six and found a table, and a few minutes later he was joined by two men. After initial pleasantries, he was asked if he had any ID with him, so they could check they had the right man.

Then they dropped the bombshell: 'I am DI Lewis and this is my colleague Sergeant Holmes. We would like you to accompany us to the local police station so that we can question you about the murder of your wife, whose body has recently been discovered in the passenger seat of a car registered to you in a lake in the Lake District.'

At the police station Brian denied involvement in the murder. When questioned further, he admitted stealing the identity of a dead man. He explained that he had been running away and took the opportunity to become someone else. He was left in a cell while checks were made with another county's police department.

When DI Lewis returned, he said, 'We have made enquiries. It is as you said. A man was found dead in a cottage a few months ago. He had been poisoned and the murderer is being sought. It was assumed, from papers found in the cottage, that the murdered man was Brian Mason, and an insurance company is preparing to pay out a significant sum to the man's widow. If you are the resurrected Mr Mason, were you party to an attempted insurance scam and are you responsible for the death of the man in the cottage? Now, I'll leave you to think. When I return you can tell me who you really are and what happened in the cottage.'

UNRELIABLE MEMORY

'Is that you, Joanne? I'm in the kitchen ironing.'

'Yes, Mum. I've got you those bits of shopping you asked me to get.'

Joanne came into the kitchen, put her shopping bag on the table and gave her mother a kiss.

'How are you today? How's the arthritis?'

'A bit painful. That's why I am sitting to iron these few things. How has your day been?'

'Not bad. I quite like it on this new ward. No new admissions and two of the dementia patients left to go into care homes. It will take them some time to adjust to their new environments, poor dears. But I did have an interesting chat with one of the dementia doctors. She mentioned one or two things that might help us with Dad.'

'What did the doctor say?'

'She said that a scrapbook with pictures of family and friends from past and present as well as familiar places might help to delay a person's memory loss. She also advised us not to assume that every new notion they come up with is make-believe. Where is Dad, by the way?'

'He is in the sitting room, reading one of his Westerns – unless he has fallen asleep. He probably thinks he's riding with the Lone Ranger or Wells Fargo.'

'Has he had any new adventures today?'

'Oh well, he has been up the garden about four times to see if he can find any eggs, even though it's more than thirty years since we kept hens. But this morning he came up with a new discovery. I asked him to post a birthday card to my sister. I thought as the postbox is only at the end of the road he surely can't get lost. Because of my arthritis I wasn't able to go with him, and there was a cold autumn wind blowing this morning.'

'Don't tell me someone found him wandering and had to bring him home.'

'No, he didn't get lost, but he didn't post the card either. He brought it back, saying he couldn't post it because someone has stolen the postbox. Whatever next! I expect he forgot why he had gone out.'

'Either that or he was looking for Wells Fargo rather than the good old GPO. Perhaps I should ask Dad about it.'

As she said this her father appeared in the doorway.

'Oh, hello, Jo. I thought I heard voices. Have you had a good day at school? Got any homework you want me to help you with?'

'Not today, Dad, thank you. I have been to work at the hospital. They wouldn't have me at school because I am too old. Remember, I had a birthday last week.'

'You remember Joanne's birthday tea, don't you, Jack?' interjected his wife.

'Yes, but how old are you?'

'I'm forty-eight now.'

'Are you? Forty-eight! Well, you are nearly as old as me. I'm only . . . um, how old am I? Would you like some eggs? I'll go and see if there are any ready.'

'It's all right, Dad. I've got some at home and there are some here for you and Mum.'

As she said this, Joanne produced a box of eggs from the shopping bag.

'Oh, you've been collecting hens' eggs.'

Joanne decided to change the subject and inquired, 'Mum tells me you couldn't find the postbox this morning, Dad.'

'What's that? Oh yes, somebody must have stolen it. I wonder if there were any letters inside. Have you heard anything about it?'

His wife then spoke: 'Well, that's the ironing done. I think we all deserve a cup of tea.'

Joanne interrupted: 'You two go into the sitting room and I'll make a pot of tea for us all.'

Joanne put the shopping away for her mother, and while the tea brewed in the pot she nipped out of the front door and went a few yards down the road so that she could see round the bend to where the postbox stood, but to her surprise it wasn't there.

She returned to the kitchen and took the tray of tea into the sitting room to find just her mother there.

'Where's Dad? He hasn't gone looking for eggs again, has he?'

'You guessed it. He'll be telling us someone's stolen the henhouse next.'

'Well, he won't be right about that, but he was right about the postbox. I've just been outside to have a look down the road, and the postbox isn't there. It reminds me of the thing the doctor advised. Just because someone is suffering from memory loss and has strange notions, don't dismiss everything they say and every idea they have, as sometimes it could be fact and not fancy.'

'Perhaps you are right. Maybe we should listen more carefully, but it is sometimes difficult to get a clue to know what he is on about, especially when the keyword is missing. Here he is now.'

Joanne's father came into the room clutching two apples in his hand. 'These were at the back of the tree and they came off easily.'

'Are they ripe?' asked Joanne.

'Probably not. They may have grubs in them.'

'What are they?'

'They're eggs. I can't remember the full name, but "eggs" is what my grandparents called them.'

'Now I understand,' cried his wife, nearly in tears of laughter: 'they are Egremont Russet apples.'

MY POLICE CELL EXPERIENCE

I have never been in a police cell before. I suppose it is a little like being in a locked waiting room. The nearest experience I have had to this is sitting in a room on my own, waiting to be called for interview. It is not too uncomfortable here even if I cannot leave or see out. At least I can sit down or even lie down if I am here for a long time. I am not in the dark and it is not cold and the room is dry. Ah! I have just noticed: the room is even equipped with masks and hand sanitiser.

I suppose I had better think why I am here and what will happen to me. What was it that the Inspector said as the door was shut? 'When I come back you can tell me your real name and what happened at the cottage.' Yes, I think those were his words, or very similar.

I guess my little adventure began when I read that book of H. G. Wells called *The History of Mr Polly*. Reading that certainly gave me the idea of running away. Mr Polly's solution to an unhappy life was to leave his home and his wife and to seek a new start.

Well, I had put up with my situation at home, where I was little more than a drudge, for far too long. I looked after the flat and did all the cooking, cleaning and laundry as well as bringing in a weekly wage, while my wife hardly spoke to me, except to demand something or tell me of the parties she went to. It didn't take more than a few months, after we married, for me to realise that she had married me for my wage packet. How on earth did I stick it for five years?

Eventually, I decided to take action. It was reading *Mr Polly* that gave me the idea, except that I didn't try to set fire to the flat or to kill myself. I thought that would be too drastic and I wasn't sure that I had the knowledge or the courage to do it. I thought I had done really well when I found that cottage with a dead man in it. Well, I didn't know there was a dead man when I went in – it was the notice about a room to rent that attracted me, and I didn't fancy sleeping outside again.

It was easy to change identities. I thought it was my lucky day when I saw that he looked quite like me and the photo in his passport was reasonably convincing. It seems now that it was not a lucky day, but a bad-luck day.

I have had the best six months since my mother died and my life changed for the worse. I like my job, my rented rooms and the people I work with. That was bad luck when one of my mates spotted that notice in the paper and suggested I might have come into money. More fool me for answering!

Now I am being investigated for killing myself, because they believe the corpse in the cottage was Brian Mason (that's my real name and who I was before I ran away). The man in the cottage was Ronald Reginald Brocklebank, it seems. And that is who the ID I showed to the Inspector states that I am now.

Oh, I have just had a thought. I suppose the body was RRB and not someone else that RRB had poisoned. Perhaps he had done an identity swap himself, before I arrived. After all, the police think that RRB had previously killed his wife by submerging his car with her in it, in a lake. I wonder what poison was used and how and when it was administered. Or did the dead man poison himself? Another thought: the notice about a room to let. Who put it there and when? I never looked for the room and . . . was there anyone else in the house when I called? Oooh, that thought is a bit eerie!

I wonder if the police have done any DNA checks. It seems it was a different investigation team that worked on the body. Someone must have identified it, because apparently there is an insurance claim about to be paid. I didn't know my life was insured. I shall have to ask the Inspector how much my wife expects to get and who has been paying the premiums. I bet she is looking forward to some exotic holidays and has probably spent some of the money on account. I think she could be in for a disappointment. (I don't think I should be rubbing my hands and smiling at the thought of her comeuppance).

I can't see how they won't charge me with some crime. I don't see how I could escape a charge. But what might it be? What are their options?

I suppose, as RRB, they could charge me with Mrs B's murder. I don't know if there is anything else that could be pinned on him unless the body turns out not to be RRB.

As Brian Mason, if they believe my story, I might be charged with identity theft, with faking my death in order to defraud the insurance company (although I don't know which company) and obtaining employment fraudulently.

Will the Inspector – now, what was his name? I know, it is Inspector Lewis and his sidekick is Sergeant Holmes. Will the Inspector tell my boss where I am and why I won't be turning up to work tomorrow?

Is there anything else they might try to pin on me? Oh – worst of all – will they charge me with the murder of RRB, or whoever he is? Perhaps the murdered man had a car, which was taken by his murderer. I only stole the bike. Oh, that's still theft, but whose bike was it?

There seem to be a lot of things I don't know. I need to write them down. Perhaps if I bang on the door someone might bring me pen and paper.

Well, it worked. The little flap in the door was opened and when I asked politely if I might have pen and paper, I was asked why I wanted them. I explained that I had been thinking, and there were so many things I wanted to talk to the Inspector about that I needed to write them down so that I wouldn't forget. Paper and pen were soon supplied, and when they were brought I took the opportunity to ask if they would let my employer know where I am and tell her it looked as though I might not be in work tomorrow.

Not knowing how long I would have, I wrote as quickly as I could. I made sure I had all my questions written down. As I put my pen down and read through what I had written, the door opened. It was as though I had completed an exam paper just in the permitted time. I almost heard my teacher say, 'Put your pens down – the time's up.'

Inspector Lewis appeared and asked if I was ready to answer his questions. I held up my paper. Without taking it, he took a quick glance, said I had been busy – almost with approval – and told me to follow him to an interview room.

In the room were Sergeant Holmes and another man, whose role seemed to be to take notes. The Inspector did the questioning, and I answered as truthfully as I could; but some questions I couldn't answer except on some occasions with a question of my own. When I asked a question, the note-taker was required to make sure he had it down.

Most of my questions they didn't answer. I think they didn't know the answers. When I asked about DNA they said they believed the body, having been identified, had been cremated. At that point Sergeant Holmes left the room. When 'Sherlock' came back into the room after phoning the other police force, he informed the Inspector in my hearing that the insurance company had asked for DNA to be taken before cremation and stored, because the sum involved was large. I got the impression that the insurance company hadn't ruled out the possibility that I might have been poisoned by my wife.

My interviewers smiled when I said that my wife had probably spent some of the insurance money on account and would be mad at me when she found out I was still alive. She probably knew I wasn't dead, but she thought I wouldn't be found.

I think they believed my story, but it didn't help them with their inquiry into the death of Mrs Brocklebank. When they took me back to my cell, I asked if I was under arrest. I was told that they could detain me for a few more hours and their colleagues from the other force would be coming to ask me questions about the dead body in the cottage. I would not be charged with any offence until that questioning had taken place.

Now I am sitting in the cell again and other thoughts come to me and more questions. What will my boss and colleagues think of me? Will I be charged, have to go to court, be sentenced and sent to prison? Will it be in the papers and will my wife and father find out where I am?

What's this? The flap has been drawn back and I have been told that I have a visitor, if I would like to talk to her. Who could it be? I hope it isn't my wife.

I'm pleased that the visitor wasn't my wife. In fact it was a very good visit and it has given me some hope that I may not come out of this too badly. I was really surprised that the visitor was my boss. She wanted to know what I was charged with and whether I had a solicitor.

I apologised for the trouble I had caused her and explained that I am not who I said I was. And then I told her my story and that I had run away and how I had been able to change my identity. I told her that I have not been charged yet, but I am to be questioned again by the police from a different county.

What she said in reply came as a shock and a surprise. She told me that she had been suspicious when I applied for the job and she wondered what sort of past I had. But she considered that my driving licence was genuine – she didn't think it had been forged. She said she liked me and the eagerness I showed to have the job. Putting me on a zero-hours contract was her insurance policy if I turned out to be a 'wrong 'un'.

Then she told me that she would tell the police that I was a good worker, liked by my colleagues and the customers. If I came out of this without being sent to prison she would continue to employ me and put the job on a proper footing. There are things to sort out, she said, and she has gone away to find a solicitor for me and to ask the Inspector if I might be released on bail.

Well, I don't think it's 'so far, so good', but it might be 'so far, not too bad . . . yet.'

Now, what are the other interrogators likely to ask? I wonder if my questions will have been passed to the other lot. Well, I still have my paper, so I can ask them again, if need be. Perhaps I can sit down, or even lie down, and think of something else. What time is it? They did leave me my watch. It is still today, just.

What a day! Think of something pleasant. I know – that young lady in the house that I delivered compost and some winter pansies to this morning for her parents. She was quite chatty and asked if I had a garden. I wonder what her name is and if I shall have to make another delivery to her mum and dad. She told me she has moved in with them for a while as they may be vulnerable if the virus comes this way again. She is part of their bubble. She was certainly bubbly. I wonder who does the gardening there and if she needs any help. Now, stop getting ideas, Brian or Ron or whoever I end up being. They can wait.

Hey, I chalked up another first – a night in a police cell. And, unlike many others who have achieved this, I didn't have to get drunk to gain admittance.

I slept quite well and I was provided with breakfast of a bacon bap and a cup of tea. As soon as I had had my breakfast the visits started. I don't know if I have become a celebrity, but everyone seemed to want to see me. Well, that's a bit of an exaggeration. I have to think of the order in which the visitors came.

Firstly, there was a young policeman with another man. The policeman was very polite. He said, 'Good morning, Mr Mason,' and then he said that, if I didn't object, the other man would take a sample for DNA testing. The other man took his sample, thanked me and said they would get the lab to process it as quickly as possible so that they could see if there is a match with my father's DNA. He said they had managed to contact my dad and he had agreed to provide his DNA. As they left, the Constable said, 'Thank you, sir. I think you can expect more questioning soon.' How about that? He called me 'sir'.

I was still reflecting on being called 'sir', when the door was opened again and 'Sherlock' came in and asked me to accompany him to the interview room. There we joined Inspector Lewis and another detective, who introduced himself. When he said his name I was flabbergasted and just had to request him to repeat it. With Sherlock – correction: Sergeant Holmes – in the same room, the last name I expected to hear was 'Inspector Moriarty'.

69

To be fair to him, he clearly appreciated my surprise and grinned as he remarked, 'It is certainly unusual for Holmes and Moriarty to be on the same side in a criminal investigation.' He then went on to point out that he was dealing with a matter of murder. He asked me questions about my visit to the cottage – particularly about dates and times. He wanted to know what I had looked at, where I had been and what I had touched. I was asked how I had arrived, how long I was there and whether I walked away. I admitted to stealing the bike. As we talked, he showed me a floorplan of the cottage and photographs and, although it was six months ago, I remembered things I had noticed on that morning but had not really registered, including the two sets of car tracks in the grass.

While I was still in the room, Moriarty suggested that there were probably two who came in one car and then took the other as a getaway vehicle. They were going to check on vehicles that had been abandoned. He also informed Inspector Lewis that they would soon know if the body was RRB as they had DNA which could be checked against that of RRB's sister, who had also come forward when she saw the advert and had been interviewed by Inspector Lewis. She was prepared to provide DNA.

They seemed to have discounted me as the murderer, because they didn't suggest they would compare my DNA with that of RRB's sister. I plucked up courage and asked how much I was insured for. I expected to hear something like £25,000, but it was ten times that figure – no wonder she wanted the dead body to be mine.

Now I am back in my cell and I have a companion. A fly made the mistake of flying through the door when it was opened, and now it is flying around from wall to wall like a demented thing, unable to find a way out. I know how you feel, Mr Fly.

I had a couple of hours sitting in that cell with nothing to do except watch the fly until he got tired of entertaining me. When the door was opened to admit another visitor the fly made a dash for it and escaped. My new visitor joined me in the cell and introduced himself as Mr Peter Lawes. He is a solicitor and was sent by Miss Gardiner, my boss. I don't know whether she ever married – she may have decided to keep her maiden name as it is so appropriate for someone who runs a garden centre. She is Miss P. Gardiner. I wonder if the P stands for Pansy or Poppy.

Mr Lawes addressed me as Mr Mason, and thereafter called me Brian. He wanted to hear my story and he said he wasn't sure whether I would face any charges – it seems that I may have been able to provide some helpful information.

It became clear that Miss Gardiner had asked Mr Lawes to see if he could find a way of straightening my life out for me. He was clearly not impressed by the behaviour of my wife – he thought it possible that the insurance company might wish to prosecute her for attempted fraud – and felt that I would have a good case for divorce. He had also spoken to my previous employers, and they had agreed to send details of my employment to him so that he could help Miss Gardiner to make my employment status with her legal in my real name.

There is one piece of the jigsaw still to fit in place. My future depends on the outcome of the DNA tests, for which the police are waiting.

I'm free! I AM FREE!

Well, I am no longer in that cell. Correction: I have left the custody suite. That's what they called it. Sounds grand, doesn't it, as though it is a prime part of a hotel?

The case is not closed. I might still be charged as I may have committed some motoring offences. Sergeant Emma Marples is considering whether I will have to pay a fixed-penalty fine or go to court.

Apparently, my DNA results show that I am Brian Mason. So they let me leave after I signed to say that I wouldn't do another runner. I noticed that Miss Gardiner has signed surety for me. Her first name is Petunia. Isn't that nice? I think it is even better than Primrose. I like petunias – they come in different colours and they are all cheerful and respectable.

It was quite late in the day when I was released from my prison, but as it is only two weeks until Christmas, many of the shops are open late. I decided to buy some Christmas cards and send one to my dad, thanking him for supplying his DNA, which has proved that I am not a murderer. I decided, eventually, to include a business card of the garden centre, so that he can contact me if he wishes.

When I returned to my rooms I received a phone call from Miss Gardiner suggesting that I should not go into work the next day, but call to see her when the centre closed for the day. When I arrived she told me she had spoken with the rest of the staff and they all wanted me to stay, although they might find it difficult for a while calling me Brian.

My first assignment the next day was a surprise. Miss Gardiner asked me to make a delivery to her parents' home. When I saw the address I recognised it: it was where I met the bubbly chatty lady. I learned that the lady is Miss Flora Gardiner, Petunia's sister. It was their parents who established the business. The order was for twenty paving slabs. I asked if Miss Flora intended to lay them herself; she replied that she was hoping to find a willing man to lay them for her. Yes, you guessed it: I shall be spending my Christmas break making a patio. I shall enjoy spending time in Miss Flora's company.

The last post before Christmas contained a card from my father with a note apologising for not being a better father and wishing me well. He also wrote that he had bumped into my wife, who had told him a tale of woe. She is facing prosecution for trying to defraud an insurance company, she has had a letter telling her that divorce proceedings have been initiated, and she is nearly £400 in arrears of rent. I think I could afford to send her £200, through Mr Lawes, to help her keep a roof over her head for a little longer.

Now, isn't that magnanimous of me! But I feel that I have got out of several prisons. In fact, I feel free.